DROPPED
IN A
CANYON

SANDRA ARDREY

authorHOUSE®

AuthorHouse™
1663 Liberty Drive
Bloomington, IN 47403
www.authorhouse.com
Phone: 1 (800) 839-8640

Published by AuthorHouse 07/01/2019

ISBN: 978-1-7283-1619-2 (sc)
ISBN: 978-1-7283-1617-8 (hc)
ISBN: 978-1-7283-1618-5 (e)

Library of Congress Control Number: 2019908101

Print information available on the last page.

Pam finally had a chance to relax after finishing the dishes and sending her boys to bed. She naps, and begins to dream…back to 1968, Charlotte, N.C.

Ahh, the comfort. There ought to be a law against having to wake in such comfort! Quiet. Too quiet. Her eyes pop open, bright, so bright. No, no, no, what time is it? The clock on the wall says it's 7:40am. A sadness came over her, which made her feel unloved and alone. The second time this week she's left home alone. Five people in this house, her father, step-mother, two step siblings and her, but no one cares enough to make sure she is up and at 'em? Well to hell with it, she thinks. School starts in 50 minutes.

She jumps up, runs to the bathroom and began filling the tub. While it's filling, she brushes her teeth and ponders what to wear. In the tub she went. The warmth and the strawberry scent of bubble bath could have sent her back to her comfort zone, but she resisted the urge. She quickly bathed and got out with 35 minutes left. Still wrapped in a towel and standing in the closet door trying to decide what to wear she did her hair in her favorite go to style, an easy, time efficient, ponytail. She finished drying off, getting the spots the air failed to touch, and grabbed her undies. She oiled down quickly. Took out her favorite skirt and a sleeveless blouse to match. The skirt was dark brown that fit her little frame just right. The blouse was yellow with big brown buttons. The shoes a brown pair of flats. Another 12 minutes had passed. She picked up her bookbag and headed for the door. Her ponytail swinging as she walked.

She saw cereal on the kitchen table, poured out a handful and ran for the door. She'd have to run a little. No problem, her weight was about 100lbs. and a fraction under 5'6", slim, with an athletic build.

1

Two blocks to go.

The late bell sounded just as she entered her first class. "You made it, congrats," said Lisa. Pam smiled at her. Lisa is her very pretty, caramel colored, sexy, best friend and has been since the 9ʰ grade. Today she was dressed in a skirt with a matching top, that had swirls going on of blue, red and yellow, in the skirt and the top. The shoes were a pair of cute sandals. This year she was wearing her hair in a curly afro. They were about the same height, but Lisa is probably a little heavier due to the fact she has more curves. They had entered the room at the same time. Lisa had been waiting for her.

Mr. Miller, their teacher, at his desk, called for attention and all homework to be passed up front. "Pamela, please collect the papers," he said.

"Yes sir," she responded. Instead of going to her desk, which is right in front of Lisa's, she stepped to the other side of the room to place down her bookbag and retrieved her own homework.

Mr. Miller is such a nice guy. Well dressed, nice body, not overly handsome just a nice fatherly, I will not take crap from you, face. He was one of the class' favorite teachers. He wore a shirt and tie every day. Everyone respected him. The only one that gave him trouble was JB. The guy that didn't care about anything, except maybe his mother showing up at school because of something he'd done, still dressed in her night clothes.

He was already dozing in class, which Mr. Miller noticed. Clack! The yardstick came down hard on the desk.

"What the hell?" shouted JB, aka Johnny Black, jumping up with his fists up, looking for a fight, who shooting?" The class busted up in laughter. Everyone was laughing and pointing. Not a good idea, she thought. He got angrier. Pam had moved to the center of the class collecting homework, but the look on JB's face had her turning and moving back to the other side of the room. The scraping and scrambling caused her to jerk her head around to see what was going on. JB was flipping over desks and knocking kids out of their chairs. By the time Mr. Miller reached him four classmates including Lisa were on

the floor. Mr. Miller grabbed him by the arm and headed for the door. Pam rushed to Lisa. She was holding her arm, She appeared to be in a lot of pain.

She jerked awake. Back to the present which was Dec. 1979, Charlotte.

Visiting the past is nothing new to her. Lately, it's becoming her thing to do. Usually it has an immediate meaning. She, at this point had no idea what an incident in their last year of high school could have to do with now. JB, she hadn't seen since that day. Lisa, however, is still her friend and lives a couple of doors down. Whatever it means will reveal itself soon enough. Of course, it could be nothing. Just a memory from the past. A place that's fine to visit, but dangerous to live in.

"Mommy, Jr. took my book."

"Pam can I fix you a night cap while I'm up?" her husband asked.

"Let me get the kids settled first," she answered.

"I just need a yes or no," said Frank.

Her husband of the last nine years has seemed a little edgy lately. She looked at him and smiled. Or rather turned up one side of her mouth, turned and walked down the hall to Franklin and Joseph, otherwise known as Frank Jr. and Joey. It was after 9:00 pm and the boys had refused to settle down. She entered the room and immediate heard "read to us mommy," they said in unison.

"Suppose I don't feel like reading?" she said.

"You do, you like to read to us because it puts us to sleep and you want us to go to sleep, right?" Her diplomatic older son of eight years says.

"And you the best mommy in the whole world," the flatterer of 7 said.

"You guys know me so well, huh?" She reached for the first book she got to, 'Tales of Mother Goose' nursery rhymes, and began reading. Although everything she read, could have been recited from memory. Things like 'Humpty Dumpty', 'Baa, Baa, Black Sheep', 'Are you Sleeping', etc. They were both asleep by page 5. She kissed them both and quietly left the room.

Frank Bradley and family lives in a nice 3 bedrooms, 2 bathrooms home. One of the bedrooms was turned into the family room. You enter, of course, into the living room which contain a deep blue very comfortable, three cushions sofa, which sat under the front window, a matching love seat, that sat perpendicular, to the front door, and a matching chair facing the love seat under the side window with a mahogany coffee table between them and in front of the sofa. The area rug covered the floor the furniture set on, it was gray and contained the blue in the sofa, brown, yellow and white, which was woven around the edges. The end tables on each end of the sofa contained beautiful lamps with a candy dish on one table and tissue and designer ashtray on the other. Even though no one smoked. The mantle over the fireplace held photos of the family and was to the right of the seating arrangement. The paintings on the walls included: snow-capped mountains, another a field of flowers on a sunny day. There was also a picture of baby angels with wings, which to her, made the room feel homey and welcoming.

The open 15X10 dining area, between the living room and kitchen set an eight-chair dining table, adorned with a colorful vase also of blue, brown, yellow and white. Usually, the table had only six chairs around it, with the two other chairs sitting strategically in the living room area. On one of the dividing walls between the living room and kitchen held a wall phone, on the kitchen's side and not visible from the living room. In the kitchen, to the left side of the house and over the sink was a window that has yellow daisies on sheer brown curtains and is in the perfect position to let in the morning sun. The sun light shining through first thing in the morning, always made Pam feel like the beginning of a perfect day. Thru the kitchen is a small hall and a bath, its colors are blue and yellow. To the right is one door to the master bedroom, and another, more in the kitchen area that goes down to the basement, where the washer and dryer is and a comfortable day bed. Their room is very spacious and is furnished with a queen size bed, a 9-drawer dresser and mirror used by Pam and a 4' high chest of drawers used by Frank in dark/cherry maple. There is also an exercise bike, used by Frank to help keep himself in shape, but also used by Pam, and a freestanding mirror, because they both loved looking their best before leaving the house. If truth be told Frank used it a little more than Pam. There are two doors to this room, one from the kitchen area and the other takes you out to a hallway that connects the bedrooms the second bathroom and the family room. To the left is the boy's room, they have bunk beds that sat side by side, two small book cases, toy boxes and dressers, one for each. Both bedrooms have lots of closet space. Back to the right, and down the short hall, to complete the circle the living room to the right, a second bath to the left, and the family room straight ahead.

In this room is the entertainment center, two sofas, and their two recliners. One sofa was at the left as you entered the room, the other on the opposite wall, under the window. Their recliners set between the sofas and directly in front of the TV.

She felt Frank coming from the kitchen as she came from the boys' room. They met at the family room. He held up two glasses. Scotch for him and vodka and juice for her. This time the smile was real as she took the glass, he held out to her. Frank is just under 5'10", and 160 lb. of hard muscles. Pam admired his beautiful smooth butterscotch toned face that inhabits light brown eyes as hypnotic as a setting sun. His full sexy lips brightens her day when he smiled and were simply made for kissing her.

"Thank you."

"You're welcome."

"You want to talk?"

"About what?"

"Whatever you want. You seem to have something on your mind," she said.

"I'm good."

"Well, you came home a little late last night. Want to tell me where you were?"

He sat there a moment saying nothing. The look on his face was one of confusion and upset. "It's not the first time I've come home late," he finally said.

"Yes, I know, but generally I know when you are going to be late and where you are."

"It's no big deal, I didn't think you'd notice," he said.

"Well last night I did. I had been thinking about you all day. Worked myself up into a frenzy after I went to bed. All I thought about was why you weren't there to poke around where no man had gone before. Yea, I noticed, there was no poking going on." She hesitantly looked up at him. He was smiling from ear to ear.

"Are you laughing at me?" she asked. They were sitting in their recliners, he leaned forward and placed a hand on her leg, "Sorry baby, if I'd known, I would have awakened you. You know I'm here for you."

"But you won't tell me where you were?"

"Nothing to tell, just out with the guys."

"You couldn't call? This is not like you. 'Seven Year Itch'?"

"No baby, nothing like that."

"Then what?"

"I don't know, when I do, then yea, we'll talk about it," he said.

"You still mine?"

"Always."

"Exclusively?"

"Won't have it any other way," he said smiling.

"Okay," I looked at my empty glass.

"You ready to go to bed?" He asked.

"Maybe I want another drink, it's Friday, no school tomorrow."

"Maybe I don't want you drunk when I go where no man has gone before me."

Pam looked into her husband's hypnotic eyes and fell under his spell. She stood.

"OK, come on pokey." She said. He laughed!

The one thing Pam absolutely adored about Frank was how he would help her clean the house on the weekend. The job he did best was the vacuuming because he moved everything with no problem. He moved beds, sofas, tables, and chairs to make sure every area was hit. Then everything was put back in its proper place. Another job was keeping the yards maintained. If Pam had another job for him, he did it without complaint.

Frank came in from outside to get a drink of water. "By the way, when do we plan to set up the Christmas tree this year?" She asked him.

"Wow! Is it that time already? Getting and setting up a tree is your call babe. Glancing at the calendar, I'd say soon." He said.

"You want to make a day of it tomorrow, with the kids. Or today?"

"Let's finish up what we are doing and then decide. What else are you planning to do?"

"Today I'm just cleaning the kitchen, what about you?"

"Only yard work, I'll be finished in maybe another hour." He said.

"I should be finished in about an hour also. OK, that would make it 1:00pm." See how the boys are dressed and let them know. We can have lunch out, right?"

"Yes, sounds good."

Saturday December 15. Perfect time to get the tree. Pam started smiling. The best time of year. The best holiday, she absolutely loved this time of year. She thought back. Ten years ago, She and Frank had started to really date. They met when she was out with someone else, that didn't work out. She had always thought of him as her knight in shining armor. Three days after they met, he called and asked her out. Almost a year later, they were married. A winter wedding, in the church he attended with his family. In a few weeks they will be celebrating their 10th anniversary together. The whole season is joyous for her.

By 1:30pm everyone was getting into the car to, first get lunch and then tree shop. The boys were as excited as she was. They had lots of questions: Where are we going to eat? How big is the tree going to be? Where are we going to put it? Can we help decorate the tree? This just brought a smile to Frank's face.

At 6:00pm they were back with a 7' tree. It was around 10:00pm before they had finished moving furniture around, decorating the tree, and sitting around watching the lights and eating sandwiches and chips. "It's so pretty, I could sit here all night," said Jr. "Yes, that would be nice, but I think we all need some sleep now," said Pam. As if on cue Frank got up, turned off the lights and ushered the boys to bed.

The next morning, they all woke up late. Too late to get to church on time. They just all had a relaxing Sunday at home. Another night was spent watching the tree and the boys writing out their Christmas lists. One was what they wanted to get, and another was what they wanted to give.

The weekend was over too quickly.

While waiting for her boys to get dressed, after helping them pick out their outfits for the day, she cleaned up the breakfast dishes. *Hot coffee and cinnamon rolls,* the thought was there and gone, in another second, *Lisa.* Lisa and cinnamon rolls, good combination, she thought.

"Come on babies, it's imperative that we depart these premises pronto." She called out. A few minutes later they came running out.

"What did you say mommy? Say it again." So, she repeated it. "Do you understand what I just said?"

"I don't understand two of the words, but I know you're saying let's get out of here now." Jr. said.

"Very good, that's exactly right, you ready?"

Her boys, she thought, were as different as night and day. While Junior was dressed in a long sleeve shirt and slacks, Joey was dressed in jeans and a colorful sweater. Both were neat and handsome as can be, but they are her children, what else would she think. The baby looked like his father and the older one looked like her. They headed for the door as they put on coats and hats. The walk to school was only 10 minutes.

The trip back took a lot longer. She ran into teachers that wanted to give a little praise to her, well behaved children. Other parents just wanted to say hello and chat a bit. It was nice. Nearly 45 minutes had passed by the time she started back. As Pam turned onto her block, she saw someone sitting on her porch. She got closer and realized it was Lisa.

"Hey, what's up girl?" Pam asked

"Got cinnamon rolls," she said.

"Well, come on in and I'll get the coffee going. Why are you out so early? You don't have to sit out here if you don't want to, you know."

"It a respect thing," said Lisa.

"OK, I get that."

"Ooh, what a beautiful tree. Not sure how my Christmas is going to be."

Lisa is a housewife, like Pam, and her husband owns his own mechanic shop. Pam has not worked since her boys were born. Lisa wants children but has not been able to get pregnant. She, like Pam, is 29 and Pam feels she has plenty of time. Her husband is a gentle giant. He's 6' and, also a very, good looking man. He has very broad shoulders, with no fat to see. A little darker than Lisa but not by much. The moustache and squared jaw line made him look almost invincible.

With the water on, Pam sat down across from her, and asked, "what's with the make-up?"

"Why, you don't like it?"

"What I don't like is the bruise underneath it. Talk to me!"

Her eyes filled with tears, sparkling like jewels in her pretty oval shaped face. Stalling, she opened the bag took out the two cinnamon rolls. She slid one to Pam and took a bite of hers. Pam got up to get the coffee.

"Well, she began, last night started out great. After dinner Leon and I watched a movie all snuggled up. We laughed, fed each other strawberries, and necked like school kids. Not necessarily in that order, just saying, it was really, nice. Then he gets a page. Afterwards, his whole mood changed, and he went to bed. I asked what was wrong. He wouldn't answer. The more I asked the angrier he got. I guess I asked one time too many, that's when he jumped up and started pushing me. I pushed back or tried to anyway. Then he hits me, with his fist on the side of my face. It would have been my nose if I hadn't seen it coming. Still it knocked me out. Can you believe that? I woke up on the floor. The lights were out so I just lay there and either went to sleep or passed out again. Next thing I hear is

Why you on the floor? He helped me up. When he saw my face he asked, what happened to you? You don't remember? A right hook. I told him."

He said, "What?" I said, "Yours!" He looked at his hand. It was a little swollen. "Guess I got me a hard head, huh?"

She hesitated for a second, while Pam sat there stunned.

"Anyway, she continued, I walked past him and went to the bathroom. I saw my face and started crying. I didn't want him to hear me, so I covered my mouth with a towel. Girl, everything went through my mind: do I tell my dad, do I call the police, do I curse him the fuck out, or wait till he's asleep and pay him back? Then I hear him crying, the kind of crying that just break your heart to hear. I walk out and he's asking why. "Why would I do that?"

"He shook his head and pulled me to him and held me a long time, repeatedly saying I don't know what happened, I don't remember, I'm sorry." "OK, I finally said. It's time for you to start getting ready for work. He says, No, I don't want to leave you. I want to know what happened. I replayed the night for him, including the page. Of course, when he checked, there was no number there. I could see he wanted to call me a liar, but he could not explain away the bruise or the swelling. Again, I suggested he get ready for work and hopefully during the day things may clear up in his mind. He finally agreed. After he left, I showered, got dressed, applied a ton of make-up, and here I am."

"Damn! When you were in the bathroom contemplating what to do, I didn't hear, tell Pam, she'll kill him. Because that's what I feel like doing." Said Pam. Lisa just smiled at her. "Except, something's off. Was he at home all night like right after work?" Pam asked.

"No, he came home over an hour later than his usual time. Said he and the guys went out for a beer."

"Yea! The boys are starting to need too much of our time."

"I know. But Frank, Leon, Clinton and Robert have been friends for forever. Boys night out was a ritual. Even before you and Frank got married. Then one day there was Bruce."

"I knew about the boys' night out. Had just never met the boys and not in too much of a hurry to meet them. Although, when you told me about this place and I fell in love with it, I knew, meeting the boys wasn't far behind. Perfect place to entertain the crew according to my husband. However, I must admit, the cookout we had was nice. I enjoyed everyone's company, except Bruce. He was cool, helpful and easy on the eyes, yet I didn't get a true feel for him. Clinton, Mr. pretty boy, on the other hand showed too many teeth. Every time I looked at him, he was grinning, creepy. No one's that happy."

"Back to you though. Are you going to be OK? Want us to drop by, call, check on things have someone beat him up before he gets home?"

Smiling, she said, "Joke all you want, I know if I picked one, you'd make sure it got done."

"Good to know you trust me. Your safety is all that matters, right now."

"You were always protective of me. Even in high school."

"That was just practice. Needed to know if what I was learning was useful stuff. Plus, the people that kept pestering you needed their ass kicked. Just because you're pretty doesn't give jealous girls or horny boys the right to push-up on you. Wish I could have gotten you in a class. Being able to defend yourself is why I continued it. Although I never had to use it much. Still, the whole thing is disturbing. Leon is a sweet guy, Right?"

"Right!"

"So why did this happen? You know what? I think you should move in here for a couple of days. You could go home get a few things, maybe even cook before you leave if you want to. Just be gone before he gets home."

"OK. I really don't want to be alone with him yet." She said, a little sad.

"Yea, we need to find out what's going on, you need to feel safe in your own home. By the way thanks for the cinnamon roll."

Franks' pager went off. He went to his office phone. He had worked for four years as a postal carrier, before getting promoted to Assistant Supervisor in mail sorting. He dialed the number.

"Hello," the voice on the other end said.

"Hey, what's up Bruce." Lately Bruce had become closer to Frank than any of the other guys.

"Just heard Leon knock Lisa out last night."

"What? Is she OK?"

"Yea, she has a bruise on her face, but the weird thing is, he doesn't remember hitting her."

"Did he tell you that? How can you do something like that and not know it?"

"That's what he told me."

"Let me call my wife. I'll talk to you later." He dialed home, but only heard the phone ringing. He hung up.

Before he left his office, his pager went off again, he recognized Robert's number his oldest friend, and called him back.

"Hello."

"Hey, what's up?" Frank, a few years younger than Robert grew up in the same neighborhood. Robert became an accountant and married his high school sweetheart Mae, also from the neighborhood. Mae works in an elementary school cafeteria. They have a sixteen-year-old daughter. They were expecting her before graduation, but not by much. They were married right after they graduation.

"Did you hear?"

"Yes, I can't believe it? I tried to call home but, didn't get an answer. So, I don't know, it sounds unbelievable."

"Could you see yourself hitting your wife?"

"No. Anyway, Pam doesn't play, she fights back."

Frank's mind went back to when he first met Pam, at a drive-in. He was with two of his buddies and he had been elected to go get refreshments. He heard this argument behind him as he was standing in line at the concession stand. He turned and saw this couple arguing. His eyes, instantly transfixed as he looked at the girl. She was stunning, he thought. The prettiest milk chocolate face he had ever laid his eyes on. Her hair was framing her face in curls that went down her back. Her slender frame was perfectly proportioned. Her sexy big, bright eyes were filled with anger and determination. Her lips, fit for a goddess, were full and luscious. Apparently, he had done something she didn't like. He was saying, 'I said I'm sorry, you can't leave, how will you get home?' and he grabbed her arm. She turned that arm in a circle forcing him to release his grip. She turned to walk away again. He caught her around the waist, lifting her up, she elbowed him in the face. He let go of her. "I am not getting back in that car, so leave me alone."

I brought you here and I'm taking you home. He started at her again. She took a fighting stance and said, 'let's see.' He reached for her and she knocked his hand away and socked him in his nose. He grabbed his nose, when he pulled his hand back there was blood. He yelled, "you stupid..."

"Say it, say it! I dare you," she said. He composed himself and rushed her, keeping his eyes on her hands, blocking when necessary, and he was able to get his arms around her. Using dead weight, she dropped through his arms. On her knees she punched him in the groin. He bent over, she stood up and punched

him on the side of his face. He fell over. He started to get up and towards her again, it was pitiful. Frank decided to step in. Really man, it's obvious she's trained. Let it go. He gave him a hand up. Look, I'll make sure she gets home if she lets me. "You can have her!" the guy said, and he was gone. He turns to her, hand extended and said "Hi, I'm Frank, and you are? "Hi, I'm Pamela." "If you want to watch the rest of the movie you can come to my car. I have two buddies with me, they can get in the back and I'll take you home afterward. You'll be perfectly safe." She thought for a second and said, "I can take the bus." "No! A pretty lady like you should not be out there on a bus. I see you can take care of yourself, but you shouldn't have to. My mom raised a gentleman, please stay. Wouldn't want him to see you out there by yourself and him behind the wheel of a car," he added as an incentive. "OK but, If I get uncomfortable, I leave." "Deal," he agreed. "Would you like something to eat, I'm buying." They got popcorn and sodas for the two of them and candy bars for dessert. The friends both wanted a hotdog and chips with a soda. They carefully arranged the food and went back to Frank's car. He made his buddy get in the back. 'This is a lady, so you guys be nice'. They watched the movie, 'The Horror of Frankenstein' to the end, and she was glad she'd stayed.

He took the guys home first. He told her he didn't want his friends to get any ideas. He drove her to the westside. They sat and talked a long time. He got her number. 'The start of a very loving relationship', he thought, as he drove away that night, smiling.

"Seriously though, I can't see any reason I would, even if I had a reason, I couldn't hit her. What about you?"

"Nah! Only a punk would hit his lady especially if it's his wife, I say walk away, but that's me."

"Have you talked to Leon?" asked Frank.

"No, Bruce told me."

"He must have called you first then, I had just hung up when you paged. Anyway, I need to get back on the floor, we'll talk later."

What a morning. Second load in the washer. First load in the dryer. A thirty-minute nap would do me good. She thought. She laid on the daybed and immediate went to sleep.

For some reason the auditorium seemed hot. Pam got this feeling that said get out, get out now. She got up to leave. The teacher said, 'please stay seated'. "Sorry, but I don't feel well, I'm about to throw up," she told the teacher. "Go, hurry back." the teacher said. She went quickly to the door leading into the school. The door on the opposite wall leads out into the yard. She walked to the very end of the hallway near the front exit and sat on the stairs leading to the second floor. A moment later she heard 'you too?' She looks up and sees another student. Didn't know his name but had seen him around. A new student. Also, a senior. 'Me too, what?'

"Felt a need to get out," he said.

"Yea, I did."

"You know why?"

"No, why?"

"You're psychic."

"Ha! I doubt it. Are you?"

"Can you keep a secret?"

"Yes, yes, I can!"

"Really? I haven't met a girl yet that could," he said.

"Well you have now! I hate gossipy people. If you tell me it's a secret, it stays a secret. So. what's your secret?"

"If you tell, I'll have to find a new school." He said

"If you do, it won't be because of me." She was looking right into his eyes.

He had come down the stairs to sit right next to her and he said, "I believe you." "I am psychic, and I know there is going to be a stampede."

"When?" she asked.

He looked at his watch. "We have time to move out of sight by going up the stairs or going outside in the yard, decide quick!" He stood. So, did she... No sooner had they turned the corner on the staircase, leading to the second floor, chaos erupted. They heard screaming, running feet, yelling and doors slamming open. She looked at him in awe.

"One question, did you do anything to cause that?" Again, they were staring each other in the eyes. "No!" he answered. She believed him. They sat out of sight of everyone, learning about each other while they waited for the calm. At the end of it all they knew each other's names, birthdays, dreams after school, and a little about family and friends. Finally, the hall was quiet. They walked out with the last of the crowd. They soon found out what had happened. Someone had left the back door to the auditorium open, and a squirrel got inside and was running and jumping all over the place. She woke.

Immediately, she remembers the last dream of Lisa being hurt. Then this morning, here she comes ...HURT!

Another blast from the past. She wondered what that one was about, unforeseen disasters or her old friend Reggie. Pam wondered if it was something to be worried about. Too many, every time she closes her eyes she dreams. She wished she could read them like Reggie, but guessed, like he says she didn't spend enough time caring about it. Anyway, all she knows is that Reggie is in California. In high school he had become a really good friend. If she wasn't with Lisa, she was with him. Now, Lisa and Reggie didn't hang together, they didn't not like each other, they just didn't care to find an interest in the other.

The nap was refreshing, now back to chores. The phone rang just as she started the dryer for the second load. As she walked away from it, she heard the phone. Running up the stairs, she got to it just as it stopped. She noticed the time. It was less than an hour before school was out. Thank God, daddy gets to pick the boys up she thought. With his new change in position on the job, he now has the honor. Time to start dinner. Remembering her house guest, she decided on smothered pork chops with broccoli, mashed potatoes, biscuits and iced tea, simple enough.

The knock on the door scared her a bit. It was loud and frantic. Quickly stepping to the window, she saw Lisa. Seeing the fear on her face she swung the door open. With a small suitcase in hand she rushed in and slammed the door shut locking it. She then walked to the dining room table and sat down. Lisa lived two doors down, walking or running was no problem.

"What's going on?"

"Leon came home early. I bolted when he went to the bathroom."

"Does he know you here? Knock. Knock. I guess that's a yes."

"Go to the basement, for now." Pam told her

Pam checked the time, 40-minutes before Frank and the boys would be home. She went to the door. Opened it, with a look that said, what the hell do you want? Apparently, the message was clear. Without a word from her, he answered.

"I'm looking for my wife!"

"Look I'm not going to lie, she's here but…"

He pushed her aside and walked in.

"Look mister, if I want you in my house, I'll invite you. Now leave!" She had walked to position between him and the kitchen.

"Where is she?" He asked.

"Probably, trembling in a corner right now. I'm sure you understand she's a little afraid of you right now."

"Yea, I get that. He said. But she knows I didn't mean it," he continued as he took a seat. Pam relaxed a little and turned back to her meal. The meat had been seasoned and was ready to be placed in a pan and in the oven. Which she proceeded to do.

"I'm sure, but that does not negate the fact that she's afraid, and did you expect to do it in the first place?" she asked him.

"No, I still don't know what happened."

"Doesn't it make sense to find out first what happened to make sure it doesn't happen again?"

"Yea, I guess." Pam was gathering dishes, pans, and silverware from her food prep area to take to the sink when she heard his pager go off. She turned towards the sink and saw a look of angry determination on his face. He stepped towards her like a zombie intending to go right through her. She dropped everything on the floor and stepped in front of him. He took one more step and she shoved her shoulder into his ribs, putting all her weight behind it, while her left hand grabbed his pager and pulled it free of his belt, he tumbled to the floor. The children were knocking on the door.

"Why you knock me down?"

"Are you OK?"

"Yea, I guess."

"Could you get the door?" I'll explain later.

When he turned to the door, she looked at the number in his pager. Went to the junk drawer, found a pencil and jotted the number down. Before anyone got to the kitchen the pager was on the floor and Pam had moved back to the sink area and was picking things up from the floor.

"What happened here," asked Frank." She turned, looked at the pager and said "Leon is that your pager?" Touching the area where his pager should have been, he said, "yea I guess it is."

"Again, what the hell is going on?" asked Frank.

When all the commotion started, Lisa had run up the stairs, when she heard Frank asking, for the second time, what's going on, she walked out.

"Sorry, it's all my fault," Lisa said.

"Guys go to your room and start your homework. I'll call you when it's time to eat. Grown folks need to talk, OK?" "OK mommy." Her little angels answered as they left the room.

"I tried to call you earlier." Frank said.

"Oh, that was you? I had just started the dryer and didn't hear the phone until I started back up. It stopped when I got to it. Sorry I missed you. What did you need?"

"Well it was involving this, sending his hand in a circle to include Leon and Lisa. I heard things and looking at your face, and your hand, looking at Lisa and Leon respectively, I guess it's true."

Leon looked down at the floor, saying, "I told her I was sorry, and I don't know how or why it happened."

"I came to talk to Pam, and she suggested I stay here until we get to the bottom of this." She said sadly.

"OK, turning to Pam he said, now explain why that mess is on the floor including Leon's pager." Everyone directed their attention to Pam.

"Well, Leon had just come in looking for his wife. I had told Lisa to go to the basement. At one point he seemed to calm down and sat down at the table. Then his pager goes off. After it went off, he stood up like he was a mad man out to destroy anything in his path. I dropped this stuff I had in my arms and stepped in front of him and shoved my shoulder in his ribs causing you to fall backwards. I guess my arm or hand struck the pager and knocked it off. Now we're all up to date."

(The thing is, thinking to herself, when she saw the look on Leon's face it scared the hell out of her. But when she dropped the pots and pans and bowls and stuff, she saw the expression change, it was like the noise brought him back to reality. Which was a blessing. At that point she had no problem shoving him, he's such a nice guy. She took the pager because she really wanted to get the number out of it. Didn't know why, but felt it was a key to what was happening.)

"Everyone sit while I finish getting dinner ready," she told them. Water was boiling on the stove, she removed it from the heat and dropped tea bags in. She then grabbed a couple of cans of cream of chicken soup and emptied them in a bowl and added two cans of cold water and mixed it together. She then grabbed from the freezer a package of broccoli and mixed some in the soup. The meat had been cooking in the oven for about 30 minutes now. She pulled the pan from the oven and flipped the meat and poured the soup mixture over the meat replaced the foil and pushed the pan back in for at least another 30 minutes. In the confusion the potatoes did not get peeled, so she put on some rice. She started her biscuits, which wouldn't take hardly any time at all. As the biscuits went in the foil came off. She heard mmm that smells good, and just smiled to herself. The sweet lemon water was taken from the freezer and the tea water was added to it. After the taste test, for the right amount of sugar and lemons it was placed back in the freezer till dinner. With the rice turned low she felt like she had a few moments to sit and join the conversation.

Lisa and Leon had been going back and forth about whether she should go home with him or not. Frank got the final word. He agreed with Pam. "Lisa should stay here until we have some idea about what's going on," but he suggested he could go home with him. Which Pam immediately vetoed, saying 'I don't think so, not tonight my friend, not tonight." They were looking at her like she had lost her mind.

"What?" she asked. Frank hid his grin. With his head down rubbing his eyebrow with one hand it allowed only Pam to see the grin on his face. "Why don't you both stay. If anything happens, we're here to intercede." Pam said.

"Time to eat. Can you guys, get the boys, and wash up to eat."

"How are you feeling?" She asked Lisa.

"Fine. I feel safe here. Even if he did stay," she said.

"By the way, you didn't leave anything on the stove, did you?"

"Not cooking, no, but the food should be put up if we're eating here."

"OK we'll send the men down to your place to do that. Honey! Can you come here a minute?"

"Yea, what's up babe?" He asked. "Could you and Leon go to their place and put their food up?

"When you get back, we eat, so hurry. First, let me have your pagers." "Why?"

"Don't want any surprises, you'll be back in no time. You won't miss them."

They gave them up. While they were gone Pam began to fix plates of food and placed them on the table. The meat on her sons' plates was cut up, but the men received two pieces of meat. She and Lisa only wanted one. The remaining meat was cut in half and poured with the soup and broccoli in a serving dish and placed on the table beside the rice and biscuits.

Everyone had just sat down at the table when Frank and Leon walked back in.

"Hey, I meant to tell you that your tree is beautiful." Said Leon.

"Thanks, let me turn it on. It really is nice, isn't it? The boys helped a lot too." Proud Frank said. Some lights were twinkling, and some were flashing. They all stared at it for a moment.

They washed their hands and joined the rest. Frank said Grace and they all said Amen and started to eat. "So, how was your day at school today?" She asked her boys.

"Good, mommy! I got a 'A' on a pop quiz in spelling. Why do they call it Pop quiz? Why not Surprise quiz, Gotcha quiz, scary quiz? Everyone was smiling. He then said, I guess I answered my own question. When you pop something like a balloon, you get all those feelings, surprise, scared, gotcha all in one, so I guess pop fits."

"You're so smart." Pam said.

"Thanks mommy."

"Well, l drew a picture," said Joey.

"Of what?" Pam asked.

"Daddy!" He said.

"Me?" Frank asked surprised

"Yes, when you was a mailman. It's hanging in the classroom. My teacher likes it."

"Really, when are we going to see this masterpiece. "

"Mommy can see it tomorrow and you can see it at the end of school."

"That's a few months away. I can't wait that long, maybe I'll stop in to see it when I pick you up tomorrow."

"That would be great daddy. You can see my other work too."

23

"Well when you do bring it home let us know, we want to see it too," said Lisa.

"OK!"

"Now a little English lesson. Jr., when to use 'a' or 'an'. You say 'an' in front of a vowel. For instants an apple, an elephant, an 'A'. In front of words that start with a consonant, you use 'a.' A book, a shoe, a house. Now there are exceptions to every rule, so pay attention when you get to it, OK? Joey, you said, when you was a mailman. The correct way would be 'you were'. Since 'you' can be used as a singular or plural pronoun. So, you are not wrong, just not grammatically correct, You will learn that later too. You guys understand?"

They both nodded. "Anybody have a rebuttal of correction?"

"Nope, sounded good to me." "I wouldn't know." "No corrections from me." Were the answers she heard.

After dinner, everyone said how much they enjoyed the dinner. Frank gave her a kiss on the cheek, and said, "Great meal babe. Let's go check-out your homework boys." He followed them to their room. Pam began to clean the kitchen with Lisa's help. While Leon was still trying to convince Lisa to come home.

"Look, you two can bunk in the family room for the night. If things go bad you have us here, and tomorrow evaluate the situation again. Tonight, let's just let it go."

"That's a good idea," Frank said as he walked in. I'm tired and you all probably are too. So, let's just settle down and relax. I for one, could use a nightcap. Anyone else?"

"Not me, Pam said, I think I want a cup of coffee and a few chocolate chip cookies."

"That's what I want too," said Lisa.

"Fix me what you're having Frank," said Leon.

With coffee and cookies in hand the ladies headed for the family room, turned on the TV, found a movie and settled in.

Frank and Leon stayed at the dinner table nursing their drinks and talking while gazing at the tree. Around 8:00pm the boys started getting loud with whatever game they were playing. Pam went in to tell them it was time to start getting ready into bed. Which meant taking baths, brushing teeth, straightening their room and getting in bed. The boys seemed tired. She got no argument. An hour later they were kissed, and the lights were out.

The four of them had watched TV for at least another hour when Frank grabbed Pam's hands and led her to their bedroom. Both men started their work day at 6:00am.

Pam felt safe leaving Lisa alone with her husband. One reason being, he's a big teddy bear, and two, the pagers were disabled in the kitchen drawer. She felt she had no reason to worry.

Frank was heading towards the shower and asked Pam if she wanted to join him.

"Maybe just long enough to wash each other's back," she told him, and gave him about 15 minutes alone time. She went in with only her robe on. The bathroom was slightly steamy, and the soap he uses, for men only, gave it a sexy feel. He was waiting for her.

Damn, this man is too sexy for words, she thought. So, before he could get his hands on her, she held up her fist with the first finger extended and said, "No! I want to get in and out. I need to get off my feet and my head on a pillar. So, turn around." He stuck out his bottom lip, dropped his hand and slowly turned around. It took everything in her to ignore his cuteness. Smiling to herself, she told him, "You continue to be a good boy, I'll give you a treat later." She could feel the excitement run through him. He stood straighter, and without seeing his face knew he was smiling. Pam had taken his washcloth and soap from him and was busy washing his back. Massaging with one hand and scrubbing with the other. Feeling the strength in his back, his shoulders, his arms is such a turn on. She turned him around to let the water rinse his back. She held him close enough to get her arms around him to make sure the soap was off. While a quickie in the shower was not out of the question, it was tonight. He had his arms around her, his eyes were pleading, his hands soothing as they caressed her. When she felt that all the soap was gone, she pushed him back and motioned for him to leave. Reluctantly, he stepped out, soaking wet (which she hated) but she did tell him to leave. With her washcloth and soap in hand she soaped her whole body and rinsed, washed and rinsed again. She then took off most of the water with her washcloth then stepped out, grabbed her robe and put in on. Frank was brushing his teeth, she moved in beside him and did the same and followed him out of the bath. Only seconds behind him, she watched that cute ass and bow legs walk back into their bedroom. Removing his towel from around his waist he threw it on the back of the chair and fell on the bed on his back. Everything was at ease. She removed her robe and started to oil her body, half way thru she turned to look at her husband and found things at attention. As she finished, she went to the foot of the bed and rubbed the remaining oil on his feet. "Is this my treat"? he asked. "Sure, she answered, and for my treat, I am going to turn off the light and when I get into bed, I want to be snoring in about 10 minutes from complete exhaustion. Understood?"

All she heard as she turned off the light was a low moan. The room went to immediate darkness. She climbed into bed and in his arms. The touch of their naked bodies coming together has always been electrifying. Tonight, was no different.

"That's the hot body I have longed for all day," she said. His mouth was exploring and his hands roaming over familiar territory felt loving and sincere. He was over her, in her, whispering her name. Making her body respond with a need she hadn't felt in a long time. A need to completely surrender to the pure raw lust of her man. She arched her back in the excitement of it all and his hands went down and grabbed her ass. Moans escaped her throat as he plunged hard and deep. Her body responding as it should with moisture and swelling. With arms clamped around his shoulders she opened, legs, heart, soul. Their rhythm was fast and fierce. Breathing increased, moans escaped from them both. His mouth was on hers his tongue buried inside gave a new sensation. She sucked with increase pleasure that rose with each heartbeat. Now, his mouth at her ear saying, "Pam, my beautiful woman, come with me. Oh, baby I love you so much, come with me. His grip tightens, come with me. Now!" They both exploded.

A few moments later Frank looked at the clock, nine minutes had passed. He smiled as he lay there listening to his wife softly snoring. She had fallen asleep nestled in his arm. But knew she would wake up turn over, grab her pillow, push up against him, and sleep till morning. Ten minutes later she did just that however, Frank didn't see it because he was sound asleep.

Her eyes popped open before the alarm went off. She got up, grabbed her robe and strutted her naked butt to the bathroom. After her shower she was ready to head to the kitchen in her robe before she remembered they had company. She went back to the room to dress. The alarm was going off. She quickly turned it off. Frank usually gets up with the second alarm. Pam found a pair of sweatpants and a t-shirt to wear, after getting dressed she went to the kitchen to prepare breakfast for family and guests. Water for coffee first, grits, eggs, bacon and toast followed.

Frank and Leon ran into each other in the hall. "Sorry man, Frank said, forgot you were here, need a towel?"

"No, I've got to get home to dress."

"Then, go to the kitchen and get something to eat, I know Pam has cooked. OK?" he said, as Frank hurried to the other bathroom.

"Good morning," Pam said, as Leon entered the kitchen, "let me fix you a plate, coffee?"

"Yes please." Lisa got up and fix his coffee just the way he likes it. Pam placed a plate of food in front of him. He ate his food and drank his coffee with gusto. "Sorry to eat and run but, I have to go home to get dressed." He started to pick up his plate, but Pam stopped him. "I got that."

"That was good Pam, thanks."

"You're welcome, go, and have a great day!"

"Thanks," he got up and kissed his wife goodbye. "Oh, can I get my pager?"

"Oh, right." She went to the drawer to get it and said, "If I were you, I wouldn't put it back together till after you are ready to leave." She took Frank's pager out, also, and set it aside. Lisa at that point had gone to take a shower and get dressed.

Frank came into the kitchen dressed and smelling good. "Good morning, my love." Said Frank.

"Good morning, darling. She responded. How are you this morning?" He wrapped his arms around her shoulders from behind. "Thank you for making today a difficult one. I will be thinking about you all day. My zipper will take a beating. What got into you, last night"?

"You! You got into me don't you remember? Seriously, though, making love with you is great. Think we'll ever get to the point when we don't want to anymore?" "Sure, he said, when we have something better to do, like watching pigs fly."

"Ha! anyway, yesterday, was mentally exhausting, but physically I needed you. So, thank you for being you."

Anytime, my love, he said and gave her a very passionate kiss that lasted a while.

"Ugh! Mommy, daddy kissing, said Joey."

"You've seen me kiss your mom before. It's what we do. You'll be lucky to find a wife one day that you enjoy kissing as much as I enjoy kissing my wife."

"You ready to eat baby?"

"Yes mommy."

"Then get your brother, you two can eat together." Pam gave Frank his coffee and started to prepare his breakfast. "Can I ask you a question?" He said.

"Of course."

"What was last night, really, about? I understand being mentally tired. But the directions, giving and following was so unbelievably satisfying. I can't tell you how much I enjoyed it. I've never seen you like that before. By the way, I didn't hurt you, did I?" he whispered.

"No, you, as always, was just right. I guess it's about what's going on, and it's a little scary. I don't know what it is but, I'm getting the feeling we haven't seen the end of it. I just needed to feel you, to feel alive in your arms to know my husband is here with me. Body and soul. I wanted to feel the love, inside and out. And you delivered, my love."

"So, you're saying no one can do what I did, right?"

"Are you fishing for a compliment, or are you serious?"

The boys walked in at that moment. "Morning mommy, daddy," said Jr. "Good morning, son," replied Frank.

"To answer your question." While trying to obstruct its' meaning from the boys by using word they, hopefully didn't know. You are right, I just don't understand why you would question it. There is no room in the right or left ventricle that isn't filled with you! As she placed food in front of the boys, she continued. The only reason you can accomplish what you do is because from the onset of this union there has been nothing but stupendous admiration, authentic affinity, unabridged respectability and an abundance of trust." As she said this, it made her realize just how much she truly loved him and depended on him to be there for her. Suddenly a fear of him not being there gripped her. Her eyes teared up and her voice trembled. He was out of his seat the moment he heard it. He rushed to her and took her in his arms and held on. Finally, he said, "I know you love me. Almost as much as I love you." That made her smile. "Don't worry, he continued I'll always be here for you. Always."

"Promise?" She asked. "Then babe, that's why this works. End of conversation?"

"Yes, end of conversation. Got to run. Love you." He kissed her lips. Turned, grabbed his pager and kissed his sons on the top of their heads. "Love you guys," he said. "Love you too daddy." They said in unison.

The boys finished their breakfast and went to get dressed for school. Lisa came in and they had a quiet breakfast together. "You want to walk with us to school?"

"No, it your time with the boys. I'll wait here."

"Ok." Pam was glad. She had someone she needed to talk to without questions from Lisa. They got to school, and she told them to hold it a minute. She turned, looking for Alice. She spotted her and had to run to catch her before she got in her car. She got close enough to call out to her, she turned, smiled and waited.

"How are you?" Asked Pam.

"Good. You? What's up?"

"I have a favor to ask."

"OK, shoot."

"I have this number and wondered if you could put a name or address to it?" Alice works at the telephone company as an operator.

"Another woman?" She asked in a tone that said I don't want to get involved.

"Heavens no! It would really surprise me if this number belonged to a woman. If you can't, I understand."

"No, no I can get it. Just promise me, it is not going to break up a happy home."

"I promise!"

"OK, give it to me. I'll have the information tomorrow."

"Great, I owe you one," and handed her the piece of paper.

She got back to the boys and said, "okay let's go see this artwork." They all walked to Joey's room. The artwork was on a billboard to the left of the room, easily seen by everyone that came in. The picture Joey drew was immediately recognized by Pam. The shock was one of disbelief. The picture was truly a masterpiece. It looked just like his father in his old uniform. "Good, huh?" The teacher said as she entered the room. "No, not good, that is magnificent. I had no idea my child has that kind of talent, look at the details in the face. This really looks like Franks. I can't wait 'till that is hanging in our home."

"If you want, you can take it, we have other works by our artist over there," said the teacher. Pam looked in the direction of her stare and felt a sense of awe at how great this little person could embrace this kind of achievement. Her heart was filled with pride and love for her little one. Her eyes misted, and Joey looked up at her and ask why she had tears in her eyes, "you don't like them?"

"Oh, honey I love them I can't begin to tell you how much."

31

"Those are happy tears," Jr. said to him. "Everything is really good. I like them too."

"Let me take my picture and get out of your way. You guys have a great day, OK?" She kissed them. They said, "you too mommy."

Back at home, Pam saw that Lisa had cleaned the kitchen and went to the family room where Lisa was watching TV. "Thanks, you didn't have to do that."

"The least I could do. What's on your agenda for today?"

First, look at this and help me decide where to put it. "Oh, my goodness, did Joey do that? That is really great!"

"I know, right?" Said Pam. For now, they decided to hang it in the boy's room.

"I have an idea. Why don't we go shopping? It's Christmas and I want to get my shopping out of the way,"

"Sounds good to me, are we going downtown?"

"Sure, why not? One bus there, one bus back." Pam went to change. She dressed in a pair of dark-gray slacks with its' matching sweater and a pair of black suede flats. Lisa was already dressed in black slacks and white sweater so the only thing she changed was her shoes. She put on a pair of black boots. They grabbed their coats and purses and were out the door.

Five hours later they were back. Pam had a black three-piece dress suit for Frank, and an art set, complete with easel for Joey. Jr. was a little harder to shop for, she had not looked at their lists, which she had meant to do, so she got him a journal and books on psychic abilities. She also got an electric train set for both. She knew she would have to shop again once she read their list. While Lisa had been looking for something to give Leon, Pam bought her a 14-carat gold necklace with matching earrings. When they joined up again, it was obvious they could not take the bus home.

They had too many bags and boxes. They had to hail a taxi. Lisa had the driver go to the back of the store to pick up her gift for Leon. Which was a portable TV that he was always saying he wanted to get for his shop. What wasn't wrapped in the store, they wrapped once they got back and placed everything under the tree. Leon and Lisa had spent the last two Christmases with Frank and Pam. This year would be the third. Leon had finally convinced Lisa to come home, so far, so good.

At the dinner table that night, Pam brought up the Christmas lists, and asked the boys to show them to her after dinner.

Pam was surprised to see that she had gotten them what was on the list, all except bikes. Daddy's department she thought. Frank agreed he would take care of that.

At the end of the week school was out for the holidays. Oh joy! Since he did not have to pick up the boys after work, Frank would go shopping. He would call Pam and tell her, depending on what he was shopping for, when to expect him.

Christmas Eve was here, Pam, expecting her guest had cleaned, and washed and made sure everyone's favorite thing was in the house. She and Lisa would not start cooking until tonight. That would be the desserts, the cornbread for the dressing, and the cobbler. Everything else will start about five in the morning.

Lisa arrived around 7:00pm, after dinner. They did not eat together on Christmas Eve. She told Pam that Frank had picked up Leon earlier and they should be back by 8:00pm. They waited for Frank and Leon around the Christmas tree. Pam and Lisa with eggnog laced with brandy and the boys with hot chocolate. At 9:00pm Pam sent the boys to get ready for bed. The girls refreshed their drinks, a little less brandy this time around, still waiting for their husbands. Around 9:45 Leon knocked on the door and ordered the ladies out of the room until further notice. Without question they went to the family room. The guys brought in boxes and bags. After making sure the boys were in bed, they brought in the bikes. It took the guys another hour to wrap their boxes and place them under the tree. Then the ladies were allowed back in the room. Frank turned on the radio in the family room, which was playing all Christmas songs. The guys made their own drinks and they all got comfortable around the tree. Pam and Frank on the sofa and Leon and Lisa on the loveseat. They talked and sang along with songs they knew. One of Pam's favorite songs came on and she jumped up and started singing to Frank 'All I want for Christmas is you'. They all applauded her at the end. A little later the soulful Luther Vandross came on with 'Every Year, Every Christmas,' Frank grabbed his wife up to the middle of the floor to dance with her, not to be outdone Leon followed suit. Frank was kissing all over Pam's neck, while Leon was asking Lisa to forgive him, for putting his hands on her. After the dance the ladies decided to get in the kitchen and start the cooking so they could all get to bed. The boys will be up sooner than we want them to be. Pam started her cornbread, and Lisa started preparing a pineapple upside down cake. Once the bread was in the oven Pam peeled apple for the cobbler she will be making. After 30 minutes in the kitchen, they heard. "I love this, said Frank. A preview of what's to come. It's smelling good ladies."

Midnight, and all was done that was going to be done tonight. They all went to bed.

As predicted, the boys were up at the crack of dawn, they were trying to be quiet, but when they saw the bikes peeking out from behind the tree, they let out a loud YAAAAAH! They then went running through the house yelling, "Merry Christmas, Merry Christmas, everybody!" That got Pam up right away, then Lisa. They gave the boys a hug and said "Merry Christmas to you too. Let's give daddy a little more time, OK?" "Let's go ahead and get dressed," she said to Lisa. They went to opposite bathrooms and showered and dressed. The guys were just getting up as they finished. Pam quickly went to the kitchen to glaze the ham and get it in the oven. She looked around and saw Frank smiling at her. "Merry Christmas, he said. "Merry Christmas, she replied. They gave each other a hug and kiss. Everyone was now up and in the living room, waiting for further instructions. "So, Pam said, how are we going to do this, one gift at a time, opened one at a time or all together?" "I vote altogether," said Lisa. "Me too," Said Jr. "I like altogether." Said Frank.

"Then, let's all get a gift with your name on it."

Gifts were opened: a watch, a pair of fur-lined gloves, ties, Legos, back-pack, and a scarf with ear- muff. Then kisses. Lisa to Leon for a very beautiful watch, Pam to Lisa for her gloves, Frank to his boys for the ties, Joey to Leon for Legos, Jr. to Lisa for the backpack, and Leon to Pam for the scarf and earmuff s. "This is what those cold morning in the shop needs, you don't know how much I appreciate this. Thanks, Pam." Next gift. Open. The boys went for their bikes. Frank opened his suit, Lisa opened her necklace and earrings, Leon opened the TV. Everyone was admiring their gift with much love, then Pam opened a trip for two to Hawaii. She screamed while dancing in place with tears falling, "What you get mommy," Joey asked. "Whatever it is, it's from daddy," said Jr. "A trip for two to Hawaii she screamed". "Who're you taking?" Asked Leon, smiling. She just stood there with her arms opened to Frank until he filled them. Jr. got busy distributing the rest of the gift to the right person. Pam took a few minutes to compose herself by checking on the ham.

The rest of the presents were opened. Joey had opened the art kit from his mom and jumped with joy, he gave her a big hug and a kiss. And he also received a backpack from Lisa that got a kiss. Jr. opened the journal with the psychic books. "Yes!" He said and kissed his mom. His last present was a mechanics' kit, especially for bikes from Leon, that got him a big hug and a thank you. Lisa had opened a spice rack from the boys and a pretty bedspread with matching sheets from Frank they all got hugs and kisses from her. Pam's last two gifts were a new purse from the boys, and Leon had gotten her a holiday festive table runner. She loved them both and gave them each a kiss. Frank's presents were cuff links from Lisa and snow chains from Leon. Just what I needed, thanks as he gave them hugs. The present Leon received from the boys was a leather wallet. "Thanks guys, how did you know the one in my pocket is falling apart? I love it." He hugged them both. Frank had to take him out back to show him his new riding lawn mower. Leon was speechless. With his larger back yard. This was what he needed. He hugged him, shook his hand, and hugged him again. "Thanks man!" The guys stayed outside a bit longer going over the ins and outs of the machine. The rest went back inside. Pam asked the boys to get rid of all the paper and take their things in their room and find places for them. While doing clean up they found another gift addressed to them. "Mommy we found another present"! "For who?" she asked. "It's for us, me and Joey." "Then open it," she said. They tore the paper off. "Wow! A train set, thanks mommy." They ran to give her a hug. "Our room is going to be crowded mom." "I know, do your best," she told them.

The ladies got busy fixing dinner. The first thing Pam did was to place the runner on the table. It was perfect. It was refolded until dinner. Which was ready about 1:00pm. The table was set with the runner and special holiday dishes. The meal included: Turkey, ham, collard greens, mac and cheese, dressing, gravy, cranberry sauce, potato salad, green bean casserole and rolls. For desserts the cake, pie and ice cream. Everyone was hungry. The excitement of opening presents had masked the hunger for a while, but it was back, and everyone was waiting anxiously to eat.

Finally, the magic words – "Wash up. Time to eat!" At the table Frank said a heart-felt prayer of thanks, for friendship, for family, and for love, health and happiness. Amen was said, but also, thank you Lord and thank you Jesus.

The conversation at dinner included the fact that nothing bad had happened in recent weeks, and how grateful they were for that. "Baby," Pam began, "did you get a bonus at work or what?" "Yes, and I wanted to spread the joy, and give gifts that keeps on giving." "Well, I think you succeeded." She said. I know I'll be thanking you forever." "Me too daddy, thank you." Said Jr.

"And thank you mommy, I think I want to paint you next," said Joey, "If it looks good then maybe I can do Leon and Lisa."

"Anytime you want, do we have to sit for it?" Lisa asked

"If you want a certain pose it would help, he replied. Or, I could do it from memory."

"That's amazing. I can't draw a circle right." Said Leon. That made Joey laugh.

"This dinner is delicious. Baby please make sure I don't eat too much, too soon." Said Frank.

"Who's going to watch me?" she said.

"Well, nobody needs to watch me, I plan to eat like a mule." Leon said. "Please pass the mac and cheese."

"Lisa, I think we out did ourselves. Leon leave room for dessert." Said Pam.

After dessert was served everyone needed a place to relax. Everyone ended up in the family room to watch a movie. Frank and Pam relaxed in their recliners. Lisa sat on the sofa under the window and Leon stretched out with his head in her lap. The boys relaxed on the other sofa. An hour into the movie all the males were asleep.

"Want a cocktail? whispered Pam. Vodka and juice?"

She nodded. Pam eased out and came back with the two drinks and gave her one.

They watched the movie to the end and waited to see what else was coming on.

"Today has been great Pam. I feel this is what Christmas is all about. Being with the ones you love. There is no one in my life closer to me than the people in this room."

"I know what you mean. I have my dad and stepmom but, like you said, the people in this room makes up my world."

"It's getting late, I think I need to get sleeping beauty here home. Does Frank work tomorrow?"

"Yes, he does, I don't know if it's all day, but he does have to go in."

"Leon too, after that meal he's going to need 9 to 10 hours sleep."

"Don't wake him yet, let me go and fix food for you to take home."

Pam went to the kitchen got the extra aluminum pans she had bought for this reason. She placed turkey and dressing in one pan, mac and cheese, slices of ham and rolls in another. She got Tupperware for the greens and one for the beans, and a smaller one for the gravy. For dessert they would just have to come visit. She placed it all in a shopping bag and went to tell her it was ready. Leon was already sitting up and Frank was awake. "Well hello, how was your nap?" she asked them both.

"More tired than before," said Leon.

"Ok, let's go sweetie. We have to get you in bed, you work tomorrow."

"The food is right by the door. If you want dessert, just stop by." They got up, Leon hugged Pam and thank her for her great hospitality. He shook Franks hand and thank him again for his present. They stumbled out, more Leon than Lisa. Lisa because he was leaning on her. At the door, Lisa grabbed the food and her presents and Leon grabbed his. I'll be by tomorrow to get the mower. "No problem," said Frank. "It's not going anywhere."

Just like that Christmas was over. A great 'New Year's Eve' was had by all. The whole gang had gathered in Leon's newly cut backyard. With plenty of drinks, food, noise makers, and firecrackers. Frank and Bruce decided they would be responsible for that. No one was to go near it or touch the fireworks. When it came time for the fireworks show, no one was disappointed they put on quite a show. At midnight everyone had a drink in their hand waiting and ready to say, "Happy New Year." The party had started at 9:00pm and ended after everyone shouted "Happy New Year" and everyone was kissed, which was around 12:15 to 12:20. With all the excitement, Pam did not think anyone else noticed how Clinton had come around twice to kiss her. She didn't like it and went to stand near Frank for the rest of the night.

The end of the week meant the end of the holidays.

School had started back up and the routine of things resumed as usual.

The boys seem to be hanging out a little more than usual. At least Pam did get an occasional phone call from Frank, telling her he would be late.

Lisa knocked around noon. "Hey girl, come on in. "How're you doing?"

"I'm good, just tired of all these nights out with the boys."

"I know" said Pam while folding clothes washed at the end of the first week of school, Pam wanted to figure out what the boys did on their nights out too. "Did I tell you the first night, a few weeks ago when Frank came in late, he wouldn't tell me where he had been? Do you know if all the guys were together?"

"I don't know."

"I'm going to call Mae when she gets home. See if there's any problems with Robert."

"What are you doing for lunch?" Asked Lisa. "We can have sandwiches and chips. What I feel like is a ham and cheese sandwich with lettuce and tomatoes, chips and soda."

"Sounds great! You got sodas?" Lisa asked.

"No."

"OK, you fix the sandwiches and I'll run get a couple of sodas."

The mom and pop store's a little beyond her house. An 8-10-minute trip.

In less time than expected Lisa came through the door in a hurry. Pam thought she acted like someone was following her, a motion of her head told Pam she was correct. Pam got to the door in time to see Clinton walk up to the door. "Hey, gorgeous! I hear you're serving lunch. Care to invite a friend in?"

"Are you serious?"

"Sure, why not? Thought maybe we could discuss the problem between the love birds." Looking past her to Lisa. The idea was tempting, maybe he could shed some light on the subject, but it just didn't feel right. Seeing him, at this time of day, in her neighborhood just felt wrong, and if nothing else she was true to her gut.

"I don't think so Clinton, I don't entertain my husband's friend when he's not home. Sorry."

"Ok, I understand, you ladies take care." He turned to leave. "But" he said, "If you want to talk you can call me and handed her a card, anytime, any reason, you can call me." The emphasizes on you. Not to appear too rude, she took it and felt his fingers slide along my hand. She pulled her hand back quickly, stepped back and closed the door. She went to the kitchen and threw the card in the drawer and washed her hands.

"Can you believe him?" Pam said.

"I know. What is he doing here? He creeped me out," said Lisa.

"Yea, me too, in more ways than one."

"I'm going to call Frank, you can start eating," I'll be right back.

She went to use the phone in the bedroom and called Frank's office. He answered quickly.

"Frank Bradly, how can I help you?"

"Stay handsome and never leave me," she replied.

"Hey babe, wow, what a nice surprise, what's up?"

"Just wanted to let you know that Clinton's in the neighborhood. Do you know why?"

"No, was he in the house?"

"No, he followed Lisa from the store, came here asking could he have lunch with us."

"And you said?" In a, just tell me everything calm tone.

"Of course, I said no, I don't entertain my husband's friend unless he's here."

"My girl. So, he left?"

"Yes."

"Well I have no idea why he was there, but that is curious." He replied.

"Yea, me and Lisa thought so too. Just wanted you to know."

"Glad you called, any problems, you know I can be home in no time."

"I know, sweetheart. We're fine. I'm going to go have some lunch now. Love you."

"Love you more! See you soon. Bye."

She went back to the kitchen to eat. Lisa was almost finished.

"You think Clinton knew anything?" Asked Pam.

"Not sure. How could he know more than our husbands? They knew nothing."

Pam decided to invite Lisa and Leon to dinner. "Maybe we can talk to them together to find out what's going on." Lisa left with the intention of bringing Leon back with her after he got home.

It was now 2:30. Everyone should be here no later than 3:45.

41

They had decided a simple dinner. Hot dogs, coleslaw and french-fries. The boys would especially like it. She also had decided, if the men didn't want it, she could throw a couple of steaks in a pan.

Lisa and Leon arrived there first. The meal was fine with him, he told them. They got to talking and only when the phone rang, did she realizes it was 4pm.

"Hello, what? I'll be right there." She hung up the phone and told them that the kids were still at school. Frank hadn't shown up. I'm going to get them. Leon offered to drive her, but she declined. I need the walk, she told him. The 10-minute walk took her 5 minutes. She was hoping Frank would be there when she got there. He wasn't. She apologized to the teacher and thanked her for waiting and calling her. The boys wanted to know where daddy was.

"I don't know." She didn't know what to think. They arrived home and still did not see his car.

When they got inside, she told the boys to wash up for dinner. While they were out of the room Pam asked Lisa to make sure the boys ate. She then asked Leon to take her to Frank's job. They left before the boys were back in the room.

"Did you talk to Frank today, at all?" She asked Leon. "No, I didn't."

They got to the Post Office and she ran inside. One of the girls she knew, Margaret, was at the counter. Good, no customers, she thought. She went to her and asked, "Margaret, do you know where Frank is?"

"I wish. We had a situation here today that only he could have handled."

"What do you mean? I know he was here, I called him, where did he go?"

"Yea, he was here, but he left at lunch and didn't come back."

"Do you know where he went?"

42

"No, but on the way out he said he might be a little late getting back, he had to help a friend."

"Who?"

"He didn't say, just rushed out."

Fear gripped her so hard she was visibly trembling. Leon put an arm around her to steady her. She let him, for a second then pushed away, saying "I'm OK thanks." Let's go. Where to now, he asked. "Home, we can call around. You call your boys and I'll call family."

Back at home, Frank Jr. jumped up as they entered the house.

"Where is daddy?" he wanted to know.

"Don't know yet, baby." She answered.

A look of sadness came over his face. "Something is wrong, daddy's in trouble."

"We don't know that yet. Did anyone call?" She looked at Lisa, she just shook her head. "Okay, you want to fix your husband something to eat while I make some phone calls?"

Her first call was to his mom and dad. Spencer, his dad answered the phone. Trying to sound ok about all of this, she said, "Frank didn't happen to come see you today, did he?"

"No, why?"

"Oh, he's a little late getting home from work. I'm sure he'll be here soon. It's just not like him not to let me know when he's going to be late."

"I'm sure you're right, but if he does stop by, I'll make sure he calls you."

"Thanks, talk to you later."

Next, she called his sister, Marlene.

"Have you seen Frank today?"

"No why?"

"He's a little late getting home, that's all."

"Well call me back when he does, I don't want to worry." "OK, I will."

She walked back to the kitchen. Leon was just finishing his meal. "Your turn, his family has not seen him."

"Ok, let's start with his best friend, Robert. Hey man, have you seen your partner today?"

"Who?"

"Frank!"

"No, why?"

"He is not home, and he should have been, more than an hour ago."

"Are you there? Is Pam freaking out?"

"Not yet, well, a little."

"We're coming over."

"Look, I'm going to call Bruce, why don't you call Clinton first, then you can let us know what he says."

"Ok, bye."

Leon called Bruce. "Hey partner, have you seen Frank today?"

"No, why?"

"He not home. Didn't come home from work."

"Doesn't he get home by 3:30 or so?"

"Yea, something like that."

"Damn, it's going on 6pm and I have not seen him. You at his house?"

"Yea."

"I'm coming over, Bye."

"I think your house is about to get filled up," he told Pam.

"Don't know if I want that…" before it was out of her mouth good there was a knock on the door. Pam opened the door to Robert and Mae. They lived on the next block over. His first words were, "Clinton saw him. He should be here in a few."

Another knock, Pam had sat down with her boys close to her on the sofa, so Leon went to the door, it was Bruce. Mae had gone to Pam explaining how they had left their daughter home doing homework, so she wouldn't be staying long, but if she needed her to come back she'd come right back, even if it was just to even out the sexes, if you know what I mean, she said looking around at Leon, Bruce and Robert.

"Yea, I know what you mean, but I think we got this," she said looking at Lisa. "Ok, keep me posted." On her way out, Clinton came in.

"So, he didn't come home, huh?" A little to smug for Pam to handle, she jumped up.

"What the hell do you mean by that?"

"Like I told Robert I saw him, but only briefly. I told him I had come by earlier and I told him how pretty you looked and how soft your skin was, he didn't like that too much. I told him, even Bruce thinks your wife is fine. You're a lucky man, I told him. I thought for sure he would go talk to Bruce. Didn't he come see you?" He asked Bruce.

With a scowl on his face Bruce said, "No, no he didn't and why would you say something like that to him? You know how he feels about his wife. By the way, what the blank do you know about her soft skin?"

"I touched it today."

"You're a lying ass dog," said Lisa.

"Ask her," he responded.

"I can't begin to tell you how much I dislike you right now, to insinuate in front of my boys that their father has any right to be upset with me because of you. You need to leave," Pam said.

"Don't we need to figure out where he is?"

"Not you. I don't want to look at you any longer much less, hear what you have to say, so leave. Leave Now!"

"Well, I think you need me. He may have said something that will tell us where he is. I can't remember right now but, something may jog my memory."

"I need to get my boys to bed. When I come back, I want you to be gone."

In their room, Frank Jr. said, "I don't like him, and I feel like he knows something but he's not going to tell you. He's evil."

Psychic abilities at work? she wondered. "What about Bruce?" "Nothing, I don't get a feeling from him, except he has secrets too. I just don't think it's about Daddy." "Well, you guys get ready for bed and I know I haven't made sure you said your prayers every night, but one for your daddy right now would be a good idea. OK?"

"We say our prayers every night. Daddy or Jr. make sure we don't forget. You want to pray with us?" Joey asked.

"Ok." They all got on their knees on the side of Jr's bed." The thing that jolted her was the fact that they were aligned with Frank's portrait that hung-over Joey bed, which was the closest to the wall. They were all looking at it with such sadness. Jr. lowered his head and he started... "Now I lay me down to sleep.... And continued with Heavenly father, wherever my dad is, please keep him safe 'till we see him again."

Joey added, "God, I love my daddy, would you let him know we love him and need him home."

Pam added, "Help us Lord, help us to cope in his absence with the assurance that he will come home safe and unharmed, Amen."

The boys clenched their mother tightly as they pour out with emotion. Wiping tears from their eyes, she kissed them, assuring them everything would be ok. Trusting their mother, they accepted her faith and kissed her as she kissed them. She then left them to their routine.

Back in the living room, she saw that Clinton was still there. "You don't hear very well, do you?"

"Can I start over please? I did say those things to Frank, but I assured him that I was joking. I realize now, to say those things in front of your children was very irresponsible. I'm sorry, very sorry, I'll apologize to them too. Those boys are Frank's world. I can't believe that I was even capable, of hurting you and your kids like that. Please forgive me. Please, I don't want to leave, especially with you hating me."

In Pam's opinion, her husband was the most handsome man alive, but looking at his friends now, she had to admit that they were all good-looking men. Robert, the oldest by about 5 years from Frank's who was 32. Robert at 37, 5'10", still had a hard body, well dressed, with a few strands of gray at the temples. He had dimples, deep and sexy. His Smile made you want to smile. Bruce, the new-bee, was 5'9" with a build smaller than the rest but still tight. He had a baby cuteness about him, with bright eyes that didn't miss much and small cute lips. Clinton was 6'1" slender with curly hair but had a veiled feel to him. Good looking and very mysterious.

"Did you think of anything that would help us?"

"Not yet." The phone rang. Pam ran to the phone like she was on fire.

"Hello, Hello?"

"Don't react, don't say a word, don't look around. Stay calm, stay very calm. Are we understanding each other?"

"Yes, we are."

"Then you know who this is, right?"

"Yes."

"This is what I want you to do. You are very tired, exhausted even. You need to rest. Everyone there, and I mean everyone, needs to leave. Tell Lisa and Lisa only to take the batteries out of Leon's pager and the phone off the hook and she'll be fine. Got it."

"Yes."

"Then say goodnight to all your guests and I'll call you back in 10-15 minutes. You can tell them that I am a teacher from school asking if you can help at school for a few hours. Can you do that?"

"Yes, I can do that."

"Good answer, bye."

"Good night."

"Who was that?" "Was that Frank?" "Was that about Frank?" The questions came at her fast. "No, it wasn't."

"Who was it?" Bruce asked. They all wanted to know.

"The school, they want me to come in, to help for a few hours tomorrow. I said yes." As she drops down on the sofa, she says, "I don't know if I am up to that. I feel so exhausted, just thinking about it. Guys I don't think we are going to get anywhere tonight. I need to sleep on this. Can we say good night 'till tomorrow? After 24 hours the police can be brought in. I appreciate all your concerns so thanks."

"No problem, we understand" said Leon. She called Lisa over and stood. She gave her a hug and whispered for her to take out the batteries and unhook the phone. You will be fine. Out loud she said, "Thanks I'll talk to you tomorrow." She hugged Leon and thank him for all his help. She turned to Robert and gave him a hug saying, "thanks for rushing to my aid, now go take care of your own family." Bruce, who had his arms out already for her, hugged her and whispered, "I want to tell you something privately, is that ok?" "Sure," she said. She started to sit when Clinton asked if she was going to give him a hug goodbye. She really didn't want to touch him and rolled her eyes. "The sooner we hug the sooner I will be out of here." "No, the sooner you get out of here the possibility of me throwing this vase lessens. I don't like you and I don't trust you. Leave, I'm going to give you till three. He stood there looking at her. She said "three," and raised her hand with the vase in it. He ran between the others. She looked at the others and lowered her other hand, as if to say get down, she got in position to really let him have it. Luckily, he saw the determination on her face and quickly escaped through the front door.

"Yelling, "I care, call me whenever."

"Wow!" Bruce said, as the others were hovering at the door, "he's really a piece of work. You guys ready to go?" They all filed out, except Bruce.

They went to the table and sat. Bruce said, "I feel I need to tell you this because of what Clinton said. That crack about even Bruce thinks you are fine. Well, first, I do think that, but second after a moment of hesitation said, I'm gay."

"Really, my husband's best friend is gay?"

"Yes, and the only reason we seem to be best friends is because he's the only one that I trusted with that information and he didn't judge. I have a femme boyfriend and Frank and I talk like we both have wives. I love him for that. My friend wanted to come with me tonight, but I told him I had to discuss it with you first. Frank wanted you to know also. He wanted to tell you but again I wanted to do it."

"Do the other guys know?"

"No, I didn't think any of them knew. But after that remark I guess they do. At least Clinton does. So now you know. Are you going to ban me from your house?"

"No, of course not. If Frank trust you, I will too. Thank you for telling me."

"Thanks for listening," he said.

"Anytime," she responded.

"Guess I better go. Wouldn't be surprised to see everyone waiting to see when I leave and wondering why I'm still here."

"The scandal!" She said, and they both started laughing. "Now you know, I'm really concerned about my buddy and my confidant, almost as much as you. I feel at a loss."

Almost is right. Thought, Pam. She felt devastated.

"I'm going to say good night now." He said and stood up. At the door she gave him another hug. No one seemed to be waiting for him. She closed the door.

She went and sat on the sofa waiting for the phone to ring. Five minutes later she heard a soft knock on the door. She went to the door. Her eyes got big and her mouth dropped open. She stepped back so he could step in. Once the door closed, they embraced.

"What! I mean when, no, why are you here."

"It seems I should have been here sooner. Before you found yourself in this situation. I felt trouble coming your way a couple of months ago. I just couldn't get a fix on where it was coming from."

"I dreamt about you the other day. I never thought, in a million years, I'd see you. How did you know where I lived, Reggie?"

"You told me, remember walking out one day turning to look back at your house, which thankfully included the house number, then directly at the street sign."

"Yes! I do. I thought, what the hell! You did that."

"Um huh. I asked you to show me your address. You did, thanks."

"You're welcome. Wow! It is so good to see you. I feel so hopeful now."

"Don't," he said.

"Why not?" she wanted to know.

"Frank is not here anymore."

"What are you saying, he's dead?"

No, in the airport, I felt him but by the time I got my bags, I didn't feel him anymore."

"So, you're saying he got on a plane? Why would he leave me, Reggie? I thought he loved me. Why? I don't understand. Was I too pushy? Too smothering? Tell me!"

"Your husband loves you very much. I don't think he left under his own volition. I think the person behind all of this is one of his friends. Did anything out of the ordinary happen, lately."

"Yes, a couple of weeks ago Lisa's husband hit her, more to the point, knocked her out. I don't know how or why but I think it has a lot to do with the pagers. I saw it for myself. One minute, Leon and I are talking calmly, his pager goes off and he became a mad man." "But then you know that, you just told me what to tell Lisa."

"I totally got it from you. I know that's how you really feel, and it feels right, at this point."

"Umm, your best friend, your husband, someone wants you all to themselves. Anyone showing extra interest in you?"

"Maybe, his friend name Clinton,"

"Clinton who?"

"I don't think I ever knew his last name."

"Is it Wills?"

"Could be, why?"

"No wonder I was blocked. That's my brother. Remember in school I never wanted to talk about my brother. He's evil."

"That's funny, Pam said, that's how my son described him."

"I would be surprised if he's not hypnotizing them."

"What do you mean you were blocked?"

"I can see into just about anyone's life, except my family. Especially if they have abilities that may surpass mine."

"Do they?" She asked. "We never tested it." He answered.

"So, what now?" she said.

"I don't know, let's sleep on it. Between the two of us we should be able to come up with something."

"Where are you staying?"

"Don't know, Can I get a room somewhere close to here?"

"Nonsense, you will stay here. You can stay in the family room or for more privacy there is the basement. There's a sofa down there and the bathroom is, come let me show you." They walked through the kitchen. "You hungry?" she asked. "Not really, what do you have to drink?" He wanted to know.

"Soft or hard?" "Soft," he replied. She said, "I have water, orange juice, iced tea, coffee."

"Iced tea would be great," he concluded. She poured him a glass, then continued to point out the bathroom and the door to the basement. Then she explained her schedule with the boys. I don't think Lisa will be here in the morning since everyone thinks I'll be at school.

"I think we should keep me quiet for a minute. Even from your children. When you take them to school I'll leave before you get back."

"No! We can have all morning to talk if you don't leave." They left it in the air. Reggie was tired, so she left him alone to get settled in.

The next morning at school Pam saw Alice waving at her. She rushed to her. Alice said, "I couldn't get a name, just an address. Hope that's enough." "That's great, thanks." Alice handed her back the piece of paper.

When Pam got back to the house, she immediately went to the basement door and called down to Reggie. She got no response. She went down and found Reggie gone. Sadly, she went back up and took out the paper Alice had given her. Good, it was an address she could easily find. She knew where it was and wondered when it would be the best time to check it out. First, she needed to get the police involved. She called the station and was transferred to 'missing person'. She told the officer the story. They needed information. They asked for name, address, license plate, age, date of birth, make and model of car and everything in between. Then the questions: Has he ever done this before? Are there any known girlfriends? Was there any trouble in the marriage? Answering no to all the questions was starting to make her angry and sad, she started crying saying, my husband and I love each other very much, he adores his boys, he has a tight network of friends, he loves his job and they love him. My husband would not just walk away from this. I need you to investigate. I want my husband. Near hysteric at this point, the officer said. We'll send someone right over.

It was four or five hours later before they got there. "Mind if we all sit down?" the officer asked. After they were all seated, they began. "It took a while Mrs. Bradley, because we already had a report on the car, so we investigated that first. The car was left at the airport with the keys still in the ignition. It had been there overnight in departure where cars are not allowed to linger, so that was priority. It is now in the police impound. They are now going over it for any signs of foul play. It is $15 a day so pick it up as soon as you can. They should be finished today. Now, do you have a photo of your husband that we can take. We have checked with his job also and know he left around 11:00am. We can check flights and see if anyone recognize him boarding a plane and to where."

"Yes," she took a picture from a frame that was sitting on the mantle.

54

"Nice looking guy. Someone should remember. Thanks, we'll get this back to you and keep you posted on our findings. OK?"

"Yes, ok and thank you very much."

The realization finally hit home. Her husband was gone. No goodbyes, no reason why. Just gone. She wondered if she'd ever see him again. She cried. Now she knew what a broken heart feels like. It literally felt like it sounded. She couldn't help but wonder if he was hurt, was he missing her and his children. Did he care. She wanted answers, her determination abated the sadness and replaced it with anger. Tonight, she was going to investigate the address. She called Lisa and got a busy signal. Phone still probably off the hook. She grabbed her purse and went to Lisa's house.

Lisa came to the door with her hair tied up and sweating. "Hey girl, what're you doing?" Pam asked.

"Cleaning! You have two boys and your house seems to stay clean. Mine is always a mess."

"Need help?" Pam wanted to know.

"No, but you can come in, I'm almost finished. Saved the kitchen for last."

"I came to ask if you can watch the boys tonight."

"Sure, what are you doing?"

"I need to investigate something."

"Did you call the police yet?"

"Yes, this is something I want to do."

Ok. By the way, Leon called and said the boys are getting together. So, he will be home late. What time you need me.

"Six would be good. Need help pulling the stove and refrigerator out?"

"You can do that?" Lisa asked surprised.

"Sure, you can walk the stove out and I'm pretty sure the frig is on wheels."

Lisa tested the frig first and found it moved with ease. When it was all the way out, she could see all the trash that had accumulated. "No wonder I could never get rid of the onion smell." She grabbed the broom and swept it out and up. She then got the mop to that area leaving it smelling nice and clean. Pam helped to push the frig back in place. Together they walked the stove away from the wall. Again trash.

"Dirtiest kitchen ever, huh?"

"Not at all, I get the same thing every 2 to 3 months when I decide to move things."

"Glad you came by." She went through the same procedure as with the frig. When finished they walked it back. She wanted to scrub the oven, but Pam suggested an ammonia and dish liquid solution. Saturate the area and let it set while she did everything else then a simple wipe down should do it. It's not like Lisa is a master baker or anything. The oven wasn't that bad. So, Lisa washed and put up dishes. She scrubbed the counter top, stove top and frig. She then wiped down the oven with no problem. Last, she mopped the rest of the floor and was done. She was so proud of her kitchen. "It looks and smells wonderful. Can't thank you enough for your help."

"You are more than welcome. I am going to go now. I am going to make a chicken casserole and fix a salad. You and Leon are more than welcome to have dinner at my house. Keep your kitchen clean a little longer."

"You convinced me, thanks."

After the salad was made and the casserole in the oven Pam went to change clothes. She wanted to be in all black. She went to get her boys. On the way back, she told them she was going out a minute and that Lisa and then Leon would be there with them.

"Don't forget to come back Mommy," said Jr.

"I won't, I'll be back in no time."

"Mommy, was someone else staying with us last night?"

"Why? Did you hear someone."

"No, not really, I kind of felt someone else in the house unfamiliar to me."

"Well yes, an old friend did stop by to see if he could help us."

"I know, it felt like a good person. I think you should listen to him."

"How do you know it was a him?"

"I don't know, I just did. Plus, you just said he. Just listen to him. Promise!"

"Ok, I promise. They got in the house and Pam asked them if they wanted to eat now and homework later, or homework now and have dinner with Lisa later."

"We can wait for Lisa, so she can have company," Jr. answered for them.

"You are such a sweet child, then go start your homework." Lisa will not be here for almost another two hours." Not wanting to get hungry later, she decided to eat something now. She got a plate, went to the frig and got a little salad then to the stove for a little of the casserole. Just as she sat down, she heard a knock. She went to the door and opened it, for Reggie. "Hey there, just getting ready to eat please join me."

"Smells good, thanks. You can fix me exactly the amount you have."

"That's not enough for a man."

"It is, because I ate earlier." She fixed his plate. "So, what have you been doing all day? Anything new?"

"No, he said, mostly driving around trying to get a feel…" She looked up and Reggie was looking over her shoulder. She turned to see her boys standing there.

"Well, come on in and meet my friend. Joey, Frank Jr, pointing as she said their names. This is Reggie, we went to high school together."

"Amazingly enough, Jr. felt you here last night. Is there a test to, you know…?"

Sure, give me a pad and a pencil. Jr. handed him pad and pencil.

"Almost like he knew you would want that," said Pam.

"I am going to write down a number, a color, a sound and a state. Now just tell me what I wrote and the order in which I wrote it." Reggie turned his back and began writing. When he finished, he folded the paper and handed it to Pam. "Ok, tell us."

Frank Jr. closed his eyes and said, "California, 17, car horn, blue." Pam opened the paper and said, "California, 17, car horn, blue." "Wow! At least I got blue right," said Pam.

"Let me do it, and I'm not telling you nothing." He placed the paper on a chair with his back to everyone he wrote bridge, confused, dirty puppy paws, at which point Reggie laughed, and last word baby. The paper was folded and given to Pam.

"Quite a list that says bridge, confused, dirty puppy paws, and baby." Pam opened the paper and again said, "Wow!" "What does it mean, Mommy?" "It means you have the gift of 'sight' you can see or sense things most of us can't."

"Your mom is also a little psychic she just doesn't trust what she sees. Between the three of us, I think we should be able to find your dad."

"Pam, I think you should hold on to those papers." Reggie said. Why? Pam wanted to know. "Psychic at work, the thoughts came from somewhere."

They started to eat again. "You guys still want to wait for Lisa"? "Yea, we'll let you two finish talking, come on Joey." "It was nice to meet you" said Jr.

"You too! See ya."

"So, when and why is Lisa coming?" Asked Reggie.

"Like you don't know."

"Humor me," he said, smiling.

"I have an address I want to check out."

'What? You're just going to go up and knock on the door?"

"Don't know yet, you want to go with me?"

"I think I have to." They finished their meal with a glass of iced tea. Pam washed up their dishes and they went and got comfortable on the sofa to wait for Lisa. "Ok so tell me what's going on in your life and don't leave out nothing."

"I got married about four years ago, we have a three-year-old daughter. My wife is a Pediatrician, I work in security. She has known about you from the moment we met. She is the best thing that could have happened to me. We are very happy together. When I saw trouble coming your way, I talked about it with her, she was the one that suggested I come and see if I could help. I was already thinking it, but she was the first to say it."

"That really says a lot about your relationship."

'What, she trusts me unconditionally, or she has a boyfriend?"

"By the smile on your face I'd say the first one. No woman in her right mind would send her husband to another woman, that, she doesn't know, unless she has complete trust in him. And knows him to be nothing but honest."

"She did say if I'm not back in a timely manner she will come looking for me."

"There it is, that's the wife talking, overflowing with love."

"I think the two of you would hit it off. The love of my life and best friend and my second, best friend. You don't mind dropping down to second place, do you?" "Not at all, if you feel for your wife like I feel for my husband, it could be no other way." Knock, Knock. "Should be Lisa now." She went to the door. It was the police.

"Can we come in a second?" "Sure, come on in." Pam said. "Just wanted to give you an update." They eyed Reggie suspiciously. "Who is this?" The one that did most of the talking, asked.

"My friend, just in from California." She answered. "Did your husband know about him?" "Yes."

"Officer, Reggie began, I'm only here for support. I left the love of my life home with our 3-year old to be here with my very close and dear friend. This is the first we've seen each other in 10yrs." "Were you ever lovers"? "No" they both said in unison.

"O.K. the good news is there was no blood found in the car. Everyone we talked to seems to like him. He's described as a nice guy, honest and hard working. Bad news, he was seen boarding an airplane headed to the west coast. The plane he got on was scheduled to make two stops. We are going to forward his picture to see if we can get further information. Understand, that if he is in another location the information will be given to you but no other action on our part will be taken. But we will alert the city to be on the lookout for him once we know where he is."

"Thank you officers, I appreciate everything you are doing." Another knock.

The police opened the door for Lisa. The quiet officer said "and this is?" "My bestfriend," she said. Lisa was eyeing Reggie the whole time and finally asked, "Where did you come from?" "Just got in really, and how are you, Lisa?"

"Good, actually glad to see you."

"Why is that." the silent one asked.

"I don't know, I guess it's because she always seemed so calm with him, like he had the ability to center her. Know what I mean?"

"No, not really." he answered.

"Maybe it was just me, a little jealous of their relationship, I guess."

"O.K. then, I think we will leave you guys to get reacquainted."

"So, did anything new happen?" Lisa asked.

"No, they don't think he was hurt, and he did get on a plane." "What, why?"

"I think only he can answer that."

"Boys wash up Lisa's here. They wanted to wait and eat with you."

"Oh, how sweet, I love it."

"We out. We will be back shortly. You left Leon a note?" Pam asked.

"Yea," Lisa said.

They left. Reggie had a blue rental car, so he drove. Which reminded Pam she had to go get their car. She directed him. When they pulled up,

Reggie said, "all you had to do was give me the address. My brother lives in this building."

"This address says it's on the third floor."

"So is my brother."

"Then let's go up," said Lisa.

"No, I want you to stay here." She started to get out and he pulled her back as she heard her son say, 'Listen to him,' and got back in the car.

"What do you want to do?" she wanted to know.

"Just give it a minute." A minute passed, and they saw the guys come out. Pam hid.

"Clinton's not with them, I'm going up. You stay right here." Reggie went up. Knocked on the door. Clinton opened the door. "Hey bro," Reggie said.

"Where the hell did you come from?" Asked Clinton.

"Your mommy, how quickly we forget. So, what's going on with you." He continued.

"Nothing," Clinton replied.

"Looks like you're having a party."

"No, had friends over, they just left."

"Glad to hear it. I'm in town for a minute thought I'd come say hello. I'll probably say goodbye on the way out. Well, you have clean-up to do, so I'll get out of your way."

"Always the perceptive one," was Clinton response.

"Always good to see you too." He held out his hand. It stayed there a for a minute.

"Really man?" Clinton, reluctantly put out his hand. There you go, he thought. They shook.

"See you." Reggie turned to leave. Clinton shut the door. The urge to run was there, so he did. He got to the car jump in and asked, "How far does Lisa live from you?" "Only two doors" she said. He took off. "What the problem?" she asked. "My brother is as evil as ever. There may be a problem at your house if we don't get there soon."

They reached her block and saw Leon walking down the street with a purpose. They pulled up beside him. "Hey Leon," she said out of the passenger side. He seemed to ignore her. Reggie drove on ahead which was only a few yards to the front of Pam's door. He got out and ran up behind Leon and placed a hand on his shoulder. Leon raised his fist to strike. Lisa blew the car horn, which turned out to be loud and ugly. Leon looked around fist still in the air, saw Pam and said "Hi." "Why is you fist in the air Leon?" She said. He looked up at it stunned. As he lowered his hand he asked, "Was I about to hit you?

"Yea, you were, I think."

"Why does this keep happening to me?"

"Do you recall being hypnotized?" asked Reggie.

"What? Who would do that?"

"Tell me step by step, what happened at Clintons' place from the time you arrived 'till the time you left." Pam was now beside them listening.

"Well, we knocked, he opened the door, we went in." Reggie interrupted with, "did you all arrive at the same time?" "No," he said, "Robert was already there."

"OK, so what happened next?"

"We went in and sat down, then Clinton started talking and …The next thing I remember we are leaving."

"So why do you go there in the first place?" Asked Reggie. "He calls us over."

"And you just go! Do you remember anything about other times you were there? Do you eat, drink, listen to music, anything?" Reggie asked. "No."

Reggie said. "Let's go inside."

Lisa had the boys at the table helping them with their homework. "Look who's going to make a great mom one day. How is it going?" said Pam.

"Hey Mommy, you find out anything? Jr wanted to know."

"No baby, not yet, still working on it. You guys almost finished?"

"Yes, I am. I'm waiting on Joey."

"What are you working on, baby?"

"My letters, I have to write them one more time."

"OK take your time."

"Let's go in the family room, she said to Reggie and Leon." As she led the way. When they were seated, Reggie and Leon on the sofa under the window, Reggie told Leon he wanted to hypnotize him to see if he could recall anything else. I can also make sure no one else can hypnotize you, if that's alright with you.

"What do you think Pam?"

"I say go for it. By the way, this is Reggie my friend from high school, and I trust him explicitly."

"OK, go ahead." "Now close your eyes. Pam, I need you to make sure we are not disturbed, by loud noises or interruptions." She left the room. She told the boys to get ready for bed as soon as Joey finish his homework and that it was imperative that they kept the noise down.

"Imperative, there is that word again. Must mean something you really have to do." Jr. surmised. "Good, to get a better understanding of the word, look it up, Ok? I'll be in later to check on you. Lisa you want to come with me?"

Pam putting her finger to her lips, they entered the room very slowly. They sat down on the sofa, near the door, to listen.

Now Leon, go back to after you entered Clinton's apartment tonight and tell me what's going on. "He put on this tape of sounds and asked if everyone was comfortable. I nodded. I guess everyone did, because I didn't hear anything. Then he said Robert, I am so proud of you, you are a very good listener. You've done all that was required of you. Bruce, very proud of you also. Leon, not so much. He touched my shoulder. For some reason you have not followed thru. Now, you all know what you are supposed to do. So, Leon you have only one more time so get it done tonight." Then the sound went off and I heard a loud clap, and we were leaving."

"So, Leon, tell me what is it that you are suppose, to do?" With a frown on his face, he said, "destroy my marriage."

"How are you suppose to do that?" "Whatever it takes to make her leave. Worse case, kill her," he said sadly.

"Do you want to do that?"

"No! I love my wife. I want children with her."

Pam looked over at Lisa. Tears were running down her cheeks. She handed her a tissue.

"Do you know why he wants you to do that?" "No."

"How long have you been meeting like this." Reggie asked.

"Maybe two to three weeks, or so."

"Do you know what was required of the others?"

"No, but the first night he told me to go home and the others went somewhere else with him."

"Was that the night you hit your wife?"

"Yes I didn't understand what I was feeling so I went to bed, only to find my wife on the floor the next morning."

"Leon, I'm going to bring you back and you will remember all that was said. If Clinton tries to hypnotize you again you will pretend to go along. It is very important for you not to react to anything you remember because we have another urgent problem to solve, and right now more information is needed. You will not get violent with him until we find Frank. Do you understand."

"Yes."

"I will count back from 5, when I get to 1, you will open your eyes and remain very calm. 5, 4, 3, 2, 1."

Leon opened his eyes and looked around. They could see his mind working as he remembered. He quietly said, "I'll kill him." He looked at his wife. Now you don't have to be afraid anymore. Just then his pager went off. Everyone held their breath watching him. "That's the signal, huh?" Everyone exhaled.

"Yes, it is." Said Reggie. "I'll get a new number tomorrow."

"It might not be necessary now. Plus, we need to keep the 'status quo' for now."

"Right now, I feel calm, like you suggested, but if he says something about me and Lisa again, I can't say what I'll do."

Pam said, "I remember Frank coming in late the other night and didn't tell me why or where he had been. Now I'm thinking that's because he probably didn't know. I think that bothered him more than it did me. Do you think he gave him a suggestion to leave town?"

"It's leaning that way," said Reggie.

"Why would he do that?"

"I think somewhere in that sick mind of his, he thinks if he gets rid of everyone close to you it would give him a chance to swoop in and save the day, and he'd become your hero."

"That is sick." said Pam.

"Not to justify anything he is doing, but he did have it a little rough. He's a good-looking man, right?"

"Yes, he alright?" said Lisa.

"Not as handsome as Frank, but yea, he's a nice-looking man." Said Pam.

"Not as good-looking as me either, but there are a lot of girls after him." Said Leon.

"I bet he doesn't see it that way. Our mom left his dad, then married mine a few years later. She hated his dad. She'd call him ugly, a misfit, a degenerate, anything she could think of. Then when she got upset with Clinton, she'd say things like, get away from me looking like that ugly dad of yours. Or, you make me sick looking like your depraved father. This went on all the time. In the beginning, he just looked hurt, later it made him angry. After a while he just took it in and showed no emotion at all. He thinks he's ugly. Now, his father is better looking than he is, but he looks just like him. He also thinks I am more handsome than he is. I know I'm not ugly, and my wife makes me feel like I'm a dream come true. So, it's not an issue, but anyone can comment on that if you like."

"The thing that makes you handsome is your self-esteem. You carry yourself like you know 'you the man', and you are. That's all a woman really wants to see. You can be the most handsome man in the room simply because you know who you are. You can handle just about any situation without coming off arrogant or loud or mean. "In other words, an intelligent, nice guy topped off with a big heart, and always weighing the good against the bad, choosing good every time is what a real man is." This came from Pam.

"OK, thanks, that's enough. One question, why didn't you fall for me?"

"You never acted like you were interested in me and I don't chase after men. Then I came to appreciate the fact that I could call you friend, and that meant a lot to me." She responded.

"Me too. As a friend I knew you'd be in my life forever. That's what I really wanted. Anyway, that's Clinton's story."

"What? Now we have to make him feel handsome?" asked Lisa

"No, don't think you can, what he needs is a professional."

Leon said, "Well I think we need to get the other guys un-hypnotize."

"You are right, we should. Whatever his problem, he can't keep manipulating these guys. We don't know what he has them doing," said Reggie.

"OK, Pam said, we can call them and have them stop by tomorrow."

"No, said Reggie, who lives the closest?" Asked Reggie.

"Robert, he lives around the corner, why?" Asked Pam.

"We need to do this now, he said. So, call Robert, ask him to stop by for a minute, make sure he comes alone." Pam went to the phone in the kitchen to call him. Robert picked up on the first ring. "Hey Robert, I need you to come over for a few minutes. I need to ask you a few personal questions. This won't take more than 15 minutes and you're back home with the family."

"Sure, I'm on my way."

The knock came quick. Mae was with him. "I told her I'd be right back, she insisted on coming." She led them to the family room. She checked on her boys. They were already asleep. She kissed them, feeling her heart beat a little faster as she realized how much she loves them. She leaves the room and sees Lisa and Leon sitting at the table, talking and holding hands. "It's probably good you came too. I am not sure what Robert can tell us, but you still need to know what it is." Pam said.

"What are we talking about here?" asked Robert.

"We know you have been hypnotized, and we want to find out why."

"Not possible," Robert said.

"It is possible. That's why Leon hit Lisa. Pam told them. So, we want to hypnotize you to see what you know and deprogram you."

"Pam, who is this?" Mae wanted to know.

"This is a friend of mine from high school and he's very good at what he does, and this is also to see if Robert may know anything about where Frank is."

"OK, if that's the case, let's get started." Robert stated like a true friend.

"You sure you want to stay?" Robert asked Mae. All she said was, "Yes."

"Here we go, Robert close your eyes." Reggie slowly took him under. "Now Robert tell me what happened at Clinton's house tonight." Robert responded the same way Leon had. He added that on other nights, other than Leon they had gone to a club.

"Tell me what you were expected to do."

"Get girls to take out their ATM card, and trick them to give us their pins. Clinton would then come over and switch the cards and leave. A little later he would return and switch the card back."

"How many girls did you do that to?"

"Maybe 3 to 4 in a night."

"Were you the only one that did that?"

"No, it was also Bruce and Frank."

"Is that all you did?" Asked Reggie."

"If he saw a girl he liked, we'd invite her back to his apartment. She would be thinking to meet one of us, when she would be meeting Clinton."

"Anything else he had you guys doing?"

"When there were two different banks to hit, he'd take one of us to do one while he went to the other.

"How much was taken?"

"$200 to $300, depending on the account, and he always wanted a receipt."

"Robert, can you think of anything else you want to share at this time. "No."

"OK Robert, when I bring you back, you will remember everything that was said. You will remain calm and not affected, this is information gained to locate Frank. Clinton will no longer be able to hypnotize you, is that clear?" "Yes."

"I will count back from 5. On 1 you will open your eyes, remember it all, and remain calm, 5...4...3...2...1."

Robert opened his eyes, after a moment a tear fell from one eye, then the other.

Reggie said, "Tell us what is making you sad."

"I looked at one of the receipts, it had only $2 left. I remember Clinton laughed. How could we have been such easy targets to an evil person like that? We have been friends for years. I can't believe this."

"That explains the perfume and lipstick." said Mae.

"You never said anything," said Robert.

"I was contemplating divorce," she said.

"But we're good right? He pleaded. Now that you know. Mae I would never cheat on you."

She smiled, "Yes, we're good, I'm glad I came."

"So now what?" Robert turning to Pam and then Reggie, asked.

"We need Bruce," said Pam. "Yes, Robert said, call him now." Pam went to the closest phone, which was in her bedroom. Bruce was there, with Ricky, 20 minutes later.

The knock on the front door brought Mae and Robert out of the family room, as Pam ushered Bruce and Ricky in. The look on their faces as they faced Leon and Lisa was 'what the hell.'

"Did you know about that?" Robert asked Leon.

"No, did you?"

"Not at all, said Robert. Frank probably did, they were always whispering about something."

"Is Frank?" Asked Mae. "Hell no, they said almost in unison. As much as he loves Pam, no way. He brags about their love life."

They brought each other up on their session. Wondering what they'd do the next time they saw Clinton face to face. Neither wanted to hurt the chance of finding Frank. Twenty minutes went by before Bruce and Ricky emerged from the room. Introductions were made. Ricky was happy to finally meet the gang and said so.

"I am so happy to meet you all. I was starting to think you were all made up, and him telling me he was with you was an excuse to traipse around. I'm so relieved my 'pooh bear' is truthful and trustworthy."

"So, 'pooh bear' what do you think about all of this," asked Leon. Everyone else laughed.

"That's Bruce to you my friend, and don't forget it. Yea, I'm gay, but I am a man and I will fight."

"Oh! that's so true, honey, this man almost knocked me down once, my 'pooh bear' knocked him silly." Clapping his hands and grinning from ear to ear. Ricky being very animated continued with, "I felt so loved and cared for, he's my hero." Bruce put his arm around Ricky, and he asked. "So, did anyone know?"

"No, we didn't did Frank?"

"Yea, he knew, he was the only one I felt I could trust enough. I didn't think you guys would understand."

"Maybe not, but you are our friend we'll take you however you come. You are good people," said Leon.

"Unlike our friend Clinton." Said Robert.

"Yea apparently, this is how he found out."

A loud knock had everyone turning to stare. "We are all here, think that's Clinton?" Asked Lisa.

"Did anyone call him," asked Pam. Everyone shook their head no. Pam went to the door. It was the police.

"We know it's late, but we saw your lights on. Can we come in?"

"Sure." She opened the door and they entered.

"Sorry to interrupt the party. It seems your husband has popped up on another case we have. Theft. Video cam caught him taking money from an AMT belonging to one of the victims. Another cam caught a Clinton Wills. Do you know him?"

"Yes. Pam said. That is why we are here, discussing what he was doing. Would you like to sit?" They took a seat. "Reggie would you like to talk about it, or should I?"

"I will, since it is my brother." A gasp came from the dining area, where the group was sitting or standing. Reggie came front and center.

"We found out tonight that Clinton was the mastermind behind all of this. He has the ability to hypnotize, which he did to all of his friends. They all were made aware of it tonight when I hypnotize them to recall past activities. While under, they each could explain everything that he had told them to do, including murder. Another gasp came from the group. But, because of the love involved, it didn't happen. They have all been deprogramed from his influence and I believe them all to be innocent of any wrong doing. Frank, however, is still missing, and still could be under a spell, for a lack of a better word, and only Clinton can possibly tell us where he is."

"How or why have you decided to be here at this particular time?" the officer asked.

"I sensed trouble in Pam's life, and I came to see if I could help. At the time I did not realize my brother was involved. I only knew she needed help."

"So, you're psychic?"

"Yes." Said Reggie.

"Then why can't you see where Frank is?"

"My abilities, like any other psychic, has limits. Plus, my connection is with Pam here, not her husband. And since Frank's connection is with my brother, makes it another block. What he is doing, why he is doing it or when, is completely out of my realm of culpability. Then there are times when I can sense things, but don't understand why, without further information. When I was at the airport, I felt a love for Pam there, but didn't understand why until I found out he was missing. Yes, even though he may not even know who he is right now, or who Pam is, the true Frank is still there."

"I see. Well, Clinton is being detained. We picked him up earlier."

"Do you think I can talk to him." Asked Reggie.

"Can you get a confession?"

"I don't know," he said. The officers looked at each other.

'Do you all confirm everything he just told us."

"Yes". "Very much so". "Everything about us, yes." "Yes we do."

"Don't understand the psychic part, but everything else, yes." Were the responses they received.

"You can come in tomorrow. Come in at 2:00pm, we will set up the observation room. You will be watched, and everything will be recorded. Do you have a problem with that?"

"No, not at all."

"Good, see you tomorrow." They got up and left. It was now 10:45 pm and everyone looked tired. "Robert, Mae don't you think your child is missing you by now?" Pam asked.

"Oh, my God! Come on Robert. Keep us posted, and Reggie, thanks." "My pleasure," he said.

"Yea, it is getting late, let's go, Ricky," said Bruce.

"Again, it's so nice to meet you all. Pam, I hope Frank comes home real soon, he sounds like a real great guy. Hug?" Pam accepted the hug. Ricky continued to say, "Stay strong girl. I can be good company too, any time you like."

"Thanks, I will remember that." She hugged Bruce and whispered, "I like him." Bruce smiled and said "Thanks, love you." They left.

Lisa walked over to her. "You good? Love you. See you tomorrow?" "You better!" They both smiled. She hugged Leon. "Take care of my girl." "Always," he said. They left. She felt sad suddenly. Reggie, sitting on the sofa, patted the seat beside him, and extended his arm. She sat down beside him allowing him to hug her while, she cried on his chest.

Reggie had stayed all night downstairs. Pam was doing a little cleaning when he came up at 1:00, dressed and ready to go. "Are you coming with me?" he asked. "I don't know. It might take more than an hour and I want to be here to pick up my boys." "It won't. I only have three or four questions, and if he can't or won't answer, we'll leave."

"OK but are you ready to leave this minute or can I change?" she asked.

"I want to leave by 1:30pm, it is now 1:06pm, you have 20 minutes."

"I'll be ready." She already knew what she was going to wear. But she wanted to rinse the sweat of the day off. She was in and out of the shower within 6 minutes. Drying herself with towel and fan took another 5 minutes. The suit she was wearing was navy blue pants, with a white top trimmed in the blue that fit like a jacket, tight around the waist and flared around the hips. The sleeves were 3 quartered and it buttoned to form a V-neck with no collar. She added earrings and a necklace. With two minutes left, she removed the rollers from her hair, she brushed the sides and ran her fingers thru the top. Her hair was permed. It was long in the top short on the side. When it looked the way she wanted it to, she gave it a quick spray. She walked out in low heels.

Reggie couldn't breathe. "Damn! He finally said. You clean up gorgeous."

"Thank you, it's time to go." she said. He followed her out, not taking his eyes off her.

"If I had come on to you, back when, would you have been receptive to it?"

"I don't know, you didn't, so let's not speculate, ok?"

"Fair enough. But I wanted to and now I wish I had. You are so pretty, inside and out."

She whirled on him. "Do I have to stay here or are you going to stop ranting?"

"Sorry, I'll stop."

"Did the door lock?" she asked.

"Yes," he answered. "Good," she responded.

He followed her around the car and opened the door for her. He then ran back around and got into the driver's seat and took off. They were at the station at 1:50pm.

They went in and was led to the room. They sat and waited. About 10 minutes later Clinton was brought in. Contrary to what he might think, Pam thought, the man was pretty. He looked at her. "Hi Pam, how you doing? You look very nice today." Pam didn't answer she just stared at him.

"Pam is just along for the ride. I'm the one that came to see you."

"So, what do you want."

"I have a couple of quick questions. One, do you know where Frank is?"

"No, no I don't," he answered.

"Then, can you figure it out?"

"No, that would be quite impossible."

"Does he know who he is?"

"Probably not."

"Why would it be impossible?" He took a deep breath.

"I know I'm being watched and probably recorded, why should I incriminate myself?"

"Because you have destroyed my family. Pam shouted. You have taken away the man that I love more than anything. She stood up. Incriminate! Incriminate! I want to kill you myself you evil, selfish, two-faced ass. Those guys trusted you and loved you like a brother and what do you do? You treat them like they are nothing, less than nothing! Can I get out of here? Because, I don't want to breathe the same air as you." She went to the door and found it locked. She started banging on it. It was opened almost immediately. She ran out.

Reggie and Clinton were watching her leave. They then turned to face each other after her departure. "Explain why it would be impossible."

"When anyone ask where he is, and I say I don't know, it's the truth isn't it?"

"Yes, I guess it is since I don't sense any deception in your answer. So, tell me how that's possible."

He leaned forward. "The guys were hypnotized right? I had them write the name of a state at the top of a sheet of paper and at the bottom the thing that would or could make them very happy. Then I cut the papers in half and switched them around. Without reading any of them, I had the papers face down, I taped two halves back together. Each sheet still had a state and a happy activity on it. They were then folded and placed in bowl. The suggestion was to go to that state and when or if he ever encountered the happy activity the spell would be erased. He sat back and said all the folded papers were then burned up."

Reggie wanted to punch him. "OK, I'm done." He stood up.

"You going to help me out of here bro?" ask Clinton.

"No, I am not. Why! Why would you do any of this?"

Clinton's eyes went to the tabletop, "I fell in love, he finally said. I didn't mean to. She is just so pretty and sexy."

"What are you talking about?"

"Her, he motioned with his head towards the door. Even you can see it. I saw it in your eyes."

"That doesn't give you the right to destroy what was clearly a perfect union. If we are lucky to find it once in our lifetime, it's a win. That kind of relationship is rare. You had no right." The door suddenly, opened, Reggie walked out as the officers came in to return Clinton back to his cell.

In the car, Pam asked. "Did you find out anything useful?" "Yea, he doesn't know and there is no way to figure it out. He destroyed any way to even begin a search." "What exactly did he say," she asked. He told her everything he had said. Including how he had fallen in love with her.

She couldn't believe it. She was so angry and hurt and frustrated and missing her husband. She was again experiencing what a broken heart felt like. She felt she couldn't breath and began to hyperventilate.

Reggie soon pulled up to the house. He jumped out and ran to her side of the car. He opened the door to help her out. He reached out a hand, she took it. As she stepped out, she collapsed in his arms. He arranged her back in the car to find her house keys. Lisa came running up, shouting. "What happen? What's wrong?"

"Boy, am I happy to see you. Could you go thru her purse and find her keys?"

"I don't have to I have my own."

"Good, grab her purse and go open the door." He lifted her in his arms and carried her inside and laid her on the sofa. He checked her heart rate and respiration and decided that a reprieve from reality right now could be a good thing.

"Doesn't she need something strong to smell to wake her up?" Said Lisa.

"How about some coffee. I could use a cup. I am sure she will to when she comes around." Lisa immediately went to the kitchen to prepare three cups of coffee.

"What time is school out." Reggie asked. Lisa looked at the clock. "Now. I'll go get the boys. Can you handle this?"

"Yea, I think I can manage."

The boys saw Lisa but not their Mom. They started crying. Frank Jr. had tears running down his face. But Joey was bawling like the baby that he is. "Where's my mommy, where's my mommy?" They cried. Lisa realized what this must look like to them. She ran to them, fell on her knees and grabbed them in a hug.

"No, no your mom is fine. She's ok. So, stop crying, everything is fine." She wiped their tears away. "Don't want your mom to feel bad that I came instead of her OK?"

"Then she's at home?"

"Yes".

"Why didn't she come?"

"Well, she didn't feel well. She overworked herself and kind of fainted. She is fine though. Come on you'll see."

"I want to run home."

"Let's get across the street first, ok?"

"OK." As soon as they crossed the street, they were both running. They got there minutes before Lisa. Luckily, Pam had come around and was drinking her coffee when the boys busted in. "What's the matter mommy?" Jr asked.

"Nothing, I'm fine."

"You going to the doctor?" He wanted to know.

"No, I don't think that's necessary." She said.

"Well, I do!" He stated.

"You do? Why?"

"I don't know, make sure you ok."

"Well a check-up might not be a bad idea, I'm due." She got up and went right to the phone.

"Dr. Morrison please," she waited a bit before the Doctor's nurse came on the line. "Can I help you?"

"Yes, I need an appointment to see the Dr."

"What is the appointment for?" the nurse asked.

"What's it for?" She repeated as she eyed the little crowd in her living room. "Check-up." Said Jr. "Stress." Said Reggie. "You fainted." Said Lisa.

"I need a check-up because I'm stressed and about an hour ago, I fainted." "Tomorrow at 10am, Yes, thank-you, see you then, bye."

At the doctor's office Pam explained to her doctor of 8 years what was going on in her life. The doctor took blood and urine and sent it to the lab 'stat'. While they waited for the results, she took her weight, checked her eyes and other vitals. After that exam, she said, "You look good, your heartbeat is strong, and your lungs sound good, but your weight is up a bit from your last visit." They went to her office where the results were waiting. She read them over and looked up at Pam with a serious face.

"What's wrong?"

"Nothing and everything. Your blood and urine came back good, you are as healthy as you can be. So, I am going to go ahead and say congratulations."

Pam's hands went to her mouth, then her eyes to try to stop the tears. "I can't do this by myself, I won't."

"You can, and you will. To finish my statement, you are pregnant. When Frank comes home and I have no doubt that he will, you can't tell him you threw away his child."

"Now, here are your prenatal prescriptions. I know it's easy to say, but keep the stress down, no overworking yourself. You are about two months I'd say but your OB/Gyn will be more precise. I am here for you whenever you need me. You have pretty babies so one more won't hurt. You hear me."

Pam smiled, despite how she felt. "I hear you," she said.

"Good."

Going home she felt close to Frank because in his car she could smell him and sitting in his seat she could imagine being in his lap. It was a peaceful feeling. One she desperately needed. *But a baby, now!* Who am I going to tell, or talk to about this? Lisa would be happy for me and sad for herself. Reggie will not be here forever. Then she remembered the lists they had guessed and decided to take another look at them.

She pulled up to the house and saw Reggie's rental. She went inside and saw him sitting at the table. "Looks like your child called it, huh?"

"What are you talking about?" As she got closer, she saw that he was already looking at the lists. "Let me see them," she said. Bridge, confused, dirty puppy paws and baby was Jr.'s list, and California, 17, car horn, blue was Reggie's. "From your list. she said, we can cross off car horn, and blue. Yes, Mr. know it all, we can cross off baby from Jr.'s."

"How do you feel about that?"

"Lonely, scared, heartbroken. On the other hand, excited, happy, looking forward, scared. Which reminds me, I need to go to his job to see if I can continue to get money. If not, I need a job. The savings will be gone in about three to four months."

"Do you want me to stay until the baby comes?"

"Heavens no! Your wife will not come looking for you because of me. Besides, I'm sure she needs you way more than I do. Plus, I have a support system. You met them all."

"Right, you have nothing to worry about. But, do you mind if I stay until after the trial?"

"Please do. I like having you here. Just make sure your wife knows the deal."

"She does, I talked to her and my child this morning." The phone rang. She got up to answer. "Hello. Sure I'd like that, see you later."

"That was Ricky. He's bored so he's coming to keep me company."

"OK, I'll excuse myself when he gets here."

"Why? You have something against the gays?"

"Of course not, your friend, your time. Anyway, do you think you can get Frank's paycheck?"

"Don't know, but I'm going to try. I'll go to the office tomorrow."

"You hungry, I am. I feel like tuna and crackers." She said.

"I could go for a little," he said. Pam made the tuna complete with hard boiled eggs, onions and celery chopped fine. She put some in a bowl surrounded by saltines. Knock Knock. Reggie grabbed his bowl and headed down stairs.

She answered the door. "Hi there, come on in. I was just fixing some tuna. Care for some?"

"No, I just ate, but you go ahead."

"Then how about something to drink?"

"I'll take a soda if you have any."

"Yes, think I'll have one too. I got some news today. Let's sit on the sofa." She fixed her bowl, rinsed the tops of the two cans of soda, gathered everything up and went to the sofa.

"So, what's up girl, dish it out."

"Well I haven't told everybody yet, so, shh with finger to her lips. Looks like we are going to add to our family. Just got back from the doctor."

"I guess it's like Frank left me something to do in his absence. Grow a baby, isn't that a hoot?"

"Ha! Girl you crazy. Any preference? You have two boys, you ready for a girl?"

"You know, it really hasn't sunk in yet. In the end, all you want is healthy."

"Well, I for one will be here for you all the way."

"Thanks, that makes me feel better all ready."

"I'm serious. I can grocery shop, put gas in the car, do heavy lifting. Not too heavy now, I am kind of delicate. You get the idea, right."

"Yes, and that's so sweet. So, what are you doing tomorrow?"

"Nothing why?"

"Will you go with me to the Post Office tomorrow?"

"Sure, you need stamps?"

"No, money."

"What!??"

The trip to the post office the next day was worth it. Between Pam's crying and Ricky animated speech about how this is a huge institution and it's not like you don't have the money. You can consider this man on a medical leave of absence. That should be good for at least 3-4 months if not 6. Because you know if he were here, he would earn every penny of it. When he comes back it's BOOM, business as usual.

"What if he's not back by…"

Ricky held up his hand like he was stopping traffic. "Then, we'll cross that bridge when we get to it."

He sat down. More calmly, he said, "If you can't do that, he has to have vacation time coming. Give the girl something. We all know if he could, Frank would be here. We are all worried about him. Don't give Pam something else to worry about like money. She, and his baby deserves your help."

The big boss said, "I'll have to take this up with corporate. We'll get back to you within the week. I am sorry for all that you are going through. Frank is an excellent employee and we like to look out for our best. So, you go take care, and I'll call you no later than next week."

In the car Pam said, "I knew it would be a good idea to take you with me. Thanks."

"Girl, no problem. I only hope I helped. You know the homophobes are no joke. Just pray none were there."

"Ha! I loved it. You were all up in their face. When you held your hand up, everybody shut the hell up. That was so funny. I almost peed on myself trying not to laugh." They both started laughing and didn't stop till they pulled up in front of the house.

When they got out, Pam threw up her hand imitating Ricky and they started laughing again.

Lisa was waiting on the porch. "What's so funny?" She said in a not so friendly tone.

"Hard to explain, you had to be there."

"Well I would have been, if I had been asked." Pam heard the hurt.

"You know what? When I got out of the car and saw you sitting here, I felt everything was going to be fine. I don't know what I'd do without you." She lifted her face with her palm under her chin and kissed her on the lips. Then took her hand and led her into the house.

Ricky, still standing in the doorway said, "do you guys want to be alone?" Pam started laughing again and said "get your ass in here. It's not like that. This is my girl, I got her back, she got mine. Plus, we all like the same things. Big strong arms and... you can fill in the rest. Mine is MIA right now, she looked at Lisa, but it's going to be alright."

"What's for lunch?"

Two months After Lock-up

Clinton had his day, in Court. He was charged with several counts of theft, a mister meaner against friends, and one charge of attempted rape.

We were all called to testify. By this time, everyone just wanted the mess to be behind them. The immediate anger had subsided, Clinton was just somebody who had to pay for his crimes. He was given 18 months for the thefts, 12 months for attempted rape and another 18 months for practicing hypnosis without credentials or permission from his subjects. Or, a fine of $1,500 for each theft victim and 12 months imprisoned. He took the latter. With time served, he'd be out in no time.

After court, Reggie left and returned to his family. He had already packed his bags and left the courthouse going to the airport. Pam had been picked up by Leon and Lisa. They dropped her off at her door, with a promise to talk much later. She had 4 hours to unwind before school was out. She entered the house and with all that had been going on, she realized she had not had a soak in a while. Something she did at least 2 to 3 times a week. She went to the bathroom and started running a bubble bath, taking advantage of the time she had now. The warm water and scented bath eased the tension and relaxed her. She dozed off.

"Pam could you come here?" said Ellen, her stepmom.

"Yea."

"I want you to clean up this mess."

"Are you kidding?"

"No, I am not!"

"The mess your 15year-old son made? You expect me to clean it up?"

"I said clean this mess up, didn't I? Now do it."

"I don't think so."

"Excuse me, you little lazy, ungrateful child. I'll beat you half to death, defying me."

"Don't think that's going to happen either. Your child your mess." She turned to leave when Ellen grabbed her hair and yanked her back. At 17 and well into her defense class, she spun around and pushed her up against the wall, pinning her there. Ellen was a tad shorter and a lot heavier which didn't matter because she knew she was stronger. Pam had her forearm under her chin and saw the fear.

"Don't ever put your hands on me again and I won't kick your ass. I am not your maid, nor am I afraid of you. You are not my mother. You just my father hoe, that he decided to marry. I don't like you and you don't like me. If you stay in your lane, I will stay in mine. While I have you here, tell me why no one thinks it's important to wake me in the morning?" She dropped her arm and stepped back. Ellen eyes went to the floor. "I don't know what you are talking about."

'Huh, you're a liar too. I'll just ask my dad."

Lisa woke with her heart beating a mile a minute. Not one of my finer moments, she thinks.

Now, how in the hell could she have fallen asleep in the tub? The water was still warm, so it couldn't have been that long. The thought worried her a bit. "That was just dumb." She said out loud. The soak lasted another 40 minutes.

Several months Later

Six weeks before the baby was due the gang decided that it was time for a baby shower. Pam, in her disassociated mind had bought nothing. The post office had shown her love and continued to send Franks check to her every two weeks. They had combined his sick pay and vacation time together and would be able to send checks for six months. That, with her friends, had her well taken care of. Leon and Lisa loved playing mom and dad, taking the boys shopping for shoes and clothes. Bruce kept them active with playing ball and running. Ricky, true to his word, picked up a grocery list every week. Every time Mae went shopping for herself, she always picked up something for Pam. No one asked for money. They showed much love to Pam. However, in her mind the true love was for her husband and what was his. She was thankful to be part of what's his.

It was getting close to noon and Pam could feel the day was going to be a hot one. It was mid-June. Being almost 8-months, she knew she was not going to be wobbling around in the back yard to long. Even though she had gained 40 lbs. everyone still wanted to tell her how radiate she was. Horse manure, she thought. She felt like an over inflated runaway balloon. No Frank, no anchor. Today like most days the questions plagued her. Was he OK? Did he have shelter, was he as lonely as she was, and the biggie, will she ever see him again? It has now been six months since she last saw him.

Knock, knock…I'll get it mommy, Jr. said as he ran from his room. "Thanks baby." Pam was on the sofa with her feet up, getting to the door was going to take a minute.

Leon and Lisa came in carrying bags and a big box. The box was placed on the floor leaning on the sofa at Pam's feet. Lisa took the other bags to the kitchen and started unloading them.

Knock, knock. Again, Jr was right there to open the door. Bruce and Ricky walked in with more bags and boxes. A minute later Robert and Mae with their daughter came in with bags and boxes.

After what she thought was everyone she said. "OK men the grill needs to be fired up. Everything you need is out there." Ricky echoed her, "Yea men, get on out there!" Everyone laughed and the three guys went out back. "What else needs to be done girl, I'm ready to help?"

"Nothing right now, you guys sit. We haven't had girl talk in a while." "Goody," Lisa said as she quickly went to squeeze between Pam and the boxes. Ricky sat in the chair closest to Pam, and Mae sat on the love seat with her back to the door.

"So, who's got news?" "I've got news", said Lisa. All eyes went to her. "Guess who's going to look like Pam in a few months?" Pam and Mae screamed. "For real" asked Pam. "About time", said Mae. Without a clue Ricky asked "Who?"

"Me!" She said directly to him.

"Oh, my goodness, this is the best news yet! Hugging her she continued with, I'm so happy for you." Then Mae hugged her and said, "You're going to make a great mom. Ricky said, "I know I'm the new guy, but what's the big deal?" "For one I have been trying for 10 year, and at 30 years old, this is my first baby."

"Oh, ok, then congrats girl, I'm very happy for you too." You must be very excited. Do you know the due date"?

"Yea, around January 12th."

"So, you're two months now." Asked Pam. "Or a little over, said Lisa. After the second miss I went to the Dr. I found out yesterday. I held it for today. Grabbing Pam's arm, she said, you don't know how hard it was for me not to run and tell you immediately, but I knew we'd all be together today, so I waited."

"Well, I don't think anyone can top that news."

Knock, knock.

Who could that be? "Mae could you get that?" "Sure."

In walked Clyde and Ellen. Pam's dad and step mom.

"Well hey, I didn't know you were coming, still trying to get up. She heard Lisa say I didn't either as she gave her a push up. She went to her dad and gave him a big hug. He gave her a loud kiss on the cheek.

"And, how are you?" she said to Ellen

"I'm doing pretty good."

"So, no word yet?" Her father wanted to know. "No, not yet."

"It's been how long and you're still waiting? I would have found a replacement by now." Said Ellen.

"Good to know, Clyde said, by the way, that was the rudest thing you could have said to her, so please apologize."

Silence.

"NOW!"

"Okay, I'm sorry, I didn't mean any harm. You are a beautiful woman, any man would love to have you, even in your present condition."

Sandra Ardrey

"Thank you??!!"

Knock, knock.

Who in the world could this be?" Clyde opened the door. Clinton walked in.

"Oh, hell no! What the hell are you doing here?" The loud anxious voice of Pam brought the men in from the back.

"What's going on? Asked Bruce, leading the group. They all laid eyes on Clinton at the same time.

"When did you get out? And what makes you think this should be your first stop?" Asked Leon.

"Let's just take him out back and work him over." Said Robert.

"I'm sorry to interrupt, but who is this?" Clyde asked Pam."

"This, motioning like a 'Let's Make a Deal' model, is the reason why my husband is not here."

"Want me to kill him? I'll go to jail. Then we can see exactly how long it takes Ellen to replace me."

"No one is going to kill anyone. People, we have children listening to this." Momentarily surprised, they all looked down at the children as if they had just materialized.

Clyde got down on one knee. "Hi, my boys,"

"Hey, grandpa." He hugged them both. Grandpa was kidding, I could never hurt another human, even if I think they deserve it. OK?"

'We know that, grandpa." Jr. said.

Pam turned to Clinton. "Explain to me why you are here, I need to know."

"I heard your baby shower was today. I talked to someone at the store down the block. She said she had heard something about it happening today, so I went shopping. I know I have expressed my regret for what happened. I just wanted to come today to say I'm sorry again to all of you. I realized sitting in that jail cell that I once had good friends and I abused it. I don't expect for you guys to except me back in the circle, because I don't deserve your trust. But I do still care for all of you. I want to do all I can to let you all know how very, very sorry I am."

"Great speech, coming from someone who told my husband to kill me." Said Lisa.

"I thought about that a lot, it made me feel miserable to think I could be so evil." I'm glad he loved you too much to follow through, even under hypnosis. That, has to make you happy to know that."

"Yea, it does."

"You welcome! Only kidding."

"Ha! the devil has jokes, said Bruce."

"Did you guys get the grill going?"

"It should be going."

"Daddy, could you check it. I'm getting hungry. Ricky, there are ears of corn, in foil, in the fridge and patties in a pan. Can you make sure those get put on the grill?"

"Bruce, the children could work up an appetite for a little while."

"Got it, come on short people."

"Lisa could I get a glass of ice-tea."

"Sure."

"Mae, there's a tablecloth for the table outside, could you get the table set up?"

"Leon, you and Robert can get the tub of beer and soda outside. There's more ice in the freezer if you need it."

Lisa returned with the tea. "Thanks, can you keep an eye on the kids. Help supervise their play."

"No, problem." She went outside.

"Mama Ellen, you can oversee everything and grab yourself a beer."

"Not a bad idea, thanks." Ellen said.

"I love the way you control things. Everyone listens and obey," said Clinton.

"Um huh, let's see how well it works on you. Seeing you here makes me extremely angry, then painfully sad. These emotions can't be good for the baby. I miss my husband, every day. I need him, I want him, and because of you, I don't have him. I need you to take your gift back and get your money, then leave us the hell alone."

"Pam, I am sorry you are hurting. It hurts me to see you in pain. Do you know how much I love you? It's making me crazy. I want to hold you and take away your pain. I can't, because I am the cause of that pain. I understand that. I went too far. Believe it or not I miss Frank too. I would bring him back tomorrow if I could. You believe me, don't you?" He touched her hand.

She just looked up at him, he had tears in his eyes. "I am so sorry. He stood, looked around to get his gift and realized a lot of the wrapping paper was the same. I can't tell which one is mine," he said. His voice trembling. She realized his dilemma.

"We'll figure it out later, you can pick it up tomorrow, unless it's a bomb, then it wouldn't matter."

"Oh, my God! I wouldn't hurt you Pam, please, I've changed. The tears were flowing now. I love you. I could never…"

Knock, knock

I'll get it. I'm going, running his hand over his face. "There's tissue over there, she pointed. He reached for one or two and dried his face. "I'll come by tomorrow. OK?"

She nodded. He bent quickly and kissed her cheek. I will never hurt you again," he said, as he touched his face to hers. He went to the door and opened it. His brother was there.

"What the!!"

"I'm leaving."

"Would you like to meet my family?" Clinton nodded, not trusting his voice.

Turning to his family he said, "This is my wife Abigail and our daughter, Crystal."

"Hey handsome, and, how are you?" Said Abigail.

"I'm good and you?" "I'm pretty good myself."

He looked down and said, "hey little niece". She said, "hey uncle Clinton".

"She is cute. He said to Reggie. You have a good-looking family. I need to go now, but Pam ask me to come back for a minute tomorrow. Maybe we can talk a little more then." He held out his hand and Reggie quickly grabbed it and held on. As Clinton walked out the door, Reggie closed it.

Pam had gotten off the sofa, anxious to give her friend a hug. He walked into her open arms. "How are you doing?" he asked.

"Good. Are you here for the baby shower?"

"Yea, we got a call, and decided right away that we wanted to be here. Plus, Abigail was anxious to meet you." At that point she turned Reggie a loose to embrace his wife. "This is great and such a nice surprise." She then turned to Crystal, and said "Hi sweetheart, you are so pretty. Let's go outside and meet everyone else," she said as she took her hand.

"I was wondering where everybody was," said Reggie. Pam lead them to the back. "Look who I found," she announced.

As she was about to take a step down, Leon was there to give her a helping hand. "Thanks" she said. When Reggie walked out the excitement was palpable. Everyone was on their feet ready to greet him with a hand shake or a hug. Even the boys were there to greet him. Jr. held out his hand, but Reggie grabbed him up in a hug, which he returned with enthusiasm. He sat him down to find Joey awaiting his turn, and, repeated the hug.

Pam asked, "Reggie do you remember my father Clyde and stepmother Ellen?" He walked over and shook hands with them both.

"Come on man, introduce your family," said Bruce.

"Wow, it's good to see you all again. This is Abigail, the love of my life. When I got home, I told her about all of you. She said the next time you go I'm going to. So, let me see if I remember all your names. Let's start easy. Pam's best friend Lisa and her husband Leon. L & L. This is Bruce, Frank's closest confidant, or the other way around, and his partner, uh, uh Ricky? Ricky gave him a thumb's up. Here are the veterans of the group, simply because they've been together the longest is Robert and Mae. He looked around for his child and saw her playing with the other children. That is Crystal getting her own introductions. So, what's new?"

Looking at Abigail, Pam said. "Looks like two new pregnancies." "Yes, my wife is one, who's the other?" Lisa raised her hand. "You too? Congratulations guys! That's great news." He turned to his wife to fill her in. "First baby after 10 years of marriage."

"Tell me, how did seeing Clinton make you feel?"

"Angry," said Leon

"Shocked," said Bruce

"Nothing, I didn't really know him," said Ricky.

"Upset, said Robert glad I didn't have my gun."

"Well if it's any consolation, I didn't sense any evilness in him, just remorse. Whether it's lasting, I don't know. So take that information as you wish."

"Guys, it's nice being out here with you, but I can't take the heat. I'm going back inside." Leon again jump up and got to the door ahead of here to help her up. There were only 2 steps, but when you can't see your feet, things can happen. She thanked him.

Pam ended up back in her favorite spot on the sofa, and, was instantly consumed with longing for her husband. Outside, Reggie asked "did Pam eat yet?"

"No, not yet, how is the food coming?" Answered Lisa. Ricky went to the grill to check on things. "It looks good," he said.

"So, let's take the party back inside and feed our guest of honor." Everyone grabbed something to take back inside. "Children let's eat." Reggie told them each to grab a water for themselves and gave each one something to take inside. Napkins, mustard, ketchup, a cup of forks and spoons, and the salt and pepper.

Lisa was able to prepare a plate for Pam. A single patty, corn on the cob, salad and chips. She squirted and little mustard and ketchup on the burger patty, Italian dressing on the salad, and a sprinkle of salt and a slab of butter on the corn. She grabbed a bottle of water and was walking to Pam when she noticed Reggie staring at her.

Mae got busy preparing plates for the children with her husband's help.

"What is it?" she asked Reggie.

"I can feel her deep in a canyon and she doesn't see a way out. She's feeling so alone without her husband." Everyone in the kitchen was now staring at her and feeling hopeless themselves.

"I think we made a good decision," said Abigail.

Reggie walked over to her. "OK, time to come up," Reggie said. "You have no idea, sometimes I get so deep my thoughts have echoes." Lisa put the food in front of her and said, that sounds so scary.

So, you want to open gifts while you eat or after, asked Mae.

"After, everyone can get something to eat, we eat together." As they turned to get food, she bit into one of her favorite foods, corn on the cob. It took her about 10 minutes to eat all she wanted. Everyone had gathered around her with their own food. Ellen and Clyde had snagged the love seat, Ricky was in the single chair and Bruce had grabbed one of the dining room chairs and sat near him. Lisa and Leon had also pulled in dining room chairs and placed them in the center to form a circle. Robert and Mae chose to stay at the table, with the children.

OK, what should I start with? She picked the biggest one, took the card off and read, "To the most beautiful woman in the world, who can only bring into the world another beautiful baby. Love Leon and Lisa". "That's so sweet, she said". She ripped the paper enough to see that it was a crib. She stood, Leon and Lisa went to her, she gave them both a kiss. She selected another box, the card said, "We both love you to death". Bruce and Ricky. She ripped the paper to find a playpen. "Love you both too." She leaned over to kiss them. They both obliged and went to her. The next card on the box said, "Thank you for being a friend. She ripped the paper and found a set a baby bottles, sitting on top of cloth diapers. "You are a good, and wise friend, thanks Mae, this was the one thing I was going to get first. I figure diapers are good to have on hand, disposables can run out at the most inopportune time. Great minds thinking alike. I love it." She sent her an air kiss. She then grabbed a bag, looked inside and saw enough baby clothes to last a year. The card said From Allison. "She picked them all out herself." Said Mae. "Really! That makes it so special." She picked up a box and looked at the card and immediately set it aside. Another bag from Ricky was a baby tub filled with all the accessories. "Wow, you guys I don't think I need to get anything else. You've covered it all."

Not everything, Robert said and handed her an envelope. Only you know how you want to feed your baby. So, this is for food and drinks. She looked in the envelope and saw a cashier check for $1200.

"Oh. my goodness, I can't take this from your family."

"I told you she would say that, said Lisa. Look, you can take it because, although this is Robert's idea, this came from everyone in this room. So, take it with all our blessings."

Pam at this point had tears flowing and dripping off her cheeks.

"I love you all with all my heart. I really don't think I'd be here if it wasn't for your friendships and love. I get lost sometime but hearing one of your voices always brings me back. I could not have asked for a better group of friends. I don't even know if I deserve this kind of love and attention. When I get my Frank back, he will know that his friends took good care of his family."

"First of all, I want to say that you are the most giving person I know. A true friend. You give your time, your expertise and your love to anyone and everyone. You deserve everything this world has to offer." Said Lisa.

"I'd like to add to that said Ricky. Being the new kid, I can tell you I have never met anyone that was as warm and open as you from the start. You make a person feel welcome and safe to be themselves. I loved you the minute I met you. So, I don't, and I know no one else here does either, want to hear you say what you don't deserve. Like Lisa said, you deserve it all."

"The one thing you deserve that we could not give you is your husband. If we could we would have made that happen not just for you but for us as well. Yea, a lot of what we did is because Frank is our friend. That doesn't take away from you. We are here because of who you are. Sweet, caring, no nonsense Pam. We all love you." Robert had stood up to tell her that.

There is one more gift, Pam, said Reggie. Obviously, it's not here.

"Before you continue, said Robert, should we assemble the furniture while we are all here to help, Pam?"

"I think you should hold off a second to hear how receptive Pam is to our gift. Pam, I feel your uncertainty in your life right now. I talked this over with my wife, and she agreed. In the first 20 minutes of meeting you, she confirmed it was a good idea. Our gift is a two story 4-bedroom house, and it's on this design. It has a staircase that goes up, right about there. He was pointing to the left side of the room. What do you say?"

"Where is this house?"

"Oh! It's in California. You would be about 15 minutes away from us by car."

Pam looked at Lisa, she saw fear in her eyes. "That sounds wonderful, but I can't leave my best friend right now."

"Okay, let's do this again. Pam? Have I ever steered you wrong?"

"No, but I love this house."

"Then listen carefully, because of your state of mind, you need a change. This change can be 3 months or 30 years. Your choice, and like I said 4-bedrooms. Leon and Lisa can join you, if you like. The downstairs, like I said is just like this. Two bedrooms to the right, living room and kitchen right here and it has a pantry. The upstairs has three rooms. One could be converted into a kitchen."

"But Leon has his own business, he can't leave, he has employees." He looked at Leon, and asked, "Are they any good?"

"One is as good as me, if not better." He said.

"Is it prosperous?" he asked. "Yes, very." He told him.

"Sell him the business, he could get a loan, buy you out and make his money back in no time." Next problem.

"What if I decide to come back in six months, what about my house?" Pam asked.

"Lease it for six months to a year."

"Schools?"

"Brand new school year with great schools. Remember the lists, there could be a great reason why this has such a strong impression on me."

"Are you sold?" She asked Lisa and Leon.

"Well, I've always wanted to visit the west coast. What do you think?"

"The more I think about it the better it sounds."

"So how long will it take for all this packing, moving furniture, selling businesses and getting plane tickets. From start to finish, how long, Reggie?" Reggie thought for a minute or two and said. "Two weeks. I can choreograph the whole thing, we can all be back in Cali before the end of June." The rest of the room was solemn. Bruce was first to speak.

"Losing two of my partners in one year is breaking my heart."

"Yea, I was looking forward to babysitting," said Ricky.

"I hate to see you all go too, thinking you may never return is killing me." Said Mae.

"So, you just gonna leave us here to deal with Clinton, said Robert.

"OK, Reggie said, first, Clinton is not to know our plan, and how about when the baby comes, you all come out for a visit. You start planning now to get your tickets and I'll take care of the room and board for three nights. Any longer and that's on you. How is that?"

"Sounds good to me, said Mae.

"To us too", said Bruce.

"When is your due date Pam"?

"August 12th."

They heard the children outside laughing and yelling at each other. It sounded like a lot of fun, but it's hot out there, thought Pam. "Lisa, could you get the children inside. Can we make sure they all get water? she said to no one in particular.

"Yea, we got this, Mae you want to help me, said Abigail. "Sure."

They went to the kitchen, washed their hands, got out the plastic cups and filled each one half full. When the children rushed in Jr. and Allison insisted on soda.

"No soda, water, ok!" "Ahh mommy," but reached for the water as instructed. After they finished Jr. and Joey ran and sat next to their mom on the sofa.

"Hello sweaty boys," she said as she kissed their foreheads. "You need baths."

"Now," they both wanted to know.

"No, later you can now go show the girls your books and play nice, both of you."

"Why do you have to say that?" Lisa asked.

"Because they each have their favorites that no one can touch without asking."

"But you teach them to share, right?"

"Children have to first learn what ownership is. If you give a child something one minute you can't expect him to want to share it the next. They shouldn't be forced to. After it's in their possession for a while and they can say 'this in mine' letting someone else enjoy it wouldn't be as much of a problem. It belongs to them they can ask for it back."

"I have so much to learn."

"Anyway, Reggie you guys are staying here, right? You can bunk in the family room. The sofa under the window lets out into a bed and the other sofa can be made up for Crystal."

"I think I'll let my girls share the bed I can bunk in the basement. I want to get a schedule going for the move. I'll be working on this all night. So, we can get a running start tomorrow. Leon can you pick me up in the morning to ride in with you?"

"Sure, I leave at 5:00am. Speaking of which, are we ready to go babe?"

"Yes, I think so, don't want to wear-out the pregnant lady." Everyone got up to leave.

"You guys go get what's left to eat and take it home, for a midnight snack, if nothing else. If anything is left on the grill, please bring that in also."

"I'll check," said Ricky. He went out and bought in the rest of the beans and corn. Pam was in the kitchen when he came in and she started fixing a plate of beans, corn, and meat patties. She asked the boys if they were hungry. They said "no."

"OK, once you say goodnight, get your baths." By 7:00pm the house was quiet. Everyone had gone to their room except Pam and Reggie. Reggie was working on the schedule and Pam was asleep on the sofa.

The next morning thing got moving. Leon's employee was thrilled with the proposition. Pam was busy talking to Real Estate Management companies and finally found one she liked. Moving companies were contacted and one was scheduled for the following weekend. Boxes were brought in along with bubble wrap and other packing necessities as needed according to Reggie. They decided on the date to leave and bought their plane tickets. The gang was called in three days before the moving van was due to start packing things like dishes, lamps, TVs, pictures, clothes, linen, towels, toys, books etc. This was done for Pam and for Leon and Lisa. Their cars were also shipped. Under Reggie direction everything was done surprising fast to Pam. Abigail just stayed out of the way, fully aware of his capabilities.

In the rental car Reggie had, on the way to the airport and their new destination Pam felt sad and hopeful. The baby was due in 4 weeks and she knew that Frank would not be by her side. She was sad for his baby as well as for herself. A baby should have his father to hold and kiss him when he enters this world, she thought. She rubbed her belly as the baby kicked And she smiled. At least you have 5 people here to greet you. You will be surrounded with love. The flight to California was smooth and uneventful.

They finally arrived at the house. It was more than she expected. The front yard had a big tree in front that shaded the porch. A lot of hot nights will be spent out here sipping tea, she thought. The street, clean and quiet, included other single-family houses. It felt like home.

Reggie had timed if perfectly. Two hours after they arrived the moving van pulled up. Although she was not allowed to do much, she was helpful in directing where things were to be placed.

It took four days to really get settled in and everything put in its place. She had just finished the lunch dishes when the phone rang.

"I'm on my way over, I need to talk to you for a second. Are you busy?"
"No, I'll be here."

The boys had gone out back to explore, and Lisa and Leon had gone back upstairs after Lisa did her part to help with the cleanup.

The doorbell rang 10 minutes after the call. Pam went to the door, opened it and said. "Hi, what's up?"

"Hey, how are you feeling today?"

"Good why?"

"I don't want you to get excited, just listen. This may be nothing at all. On my route to and from work I pass the Post office down on Central, in LA, and lately every time I go pass, I feel a connection to you. Like I said it could be nothing, I do get feelings I can't explain. In any case, I thought you deserved to know." "Thanks, I appreciate it." Reggie left.

"What was that about?" Leon wanted to know, with Lisa standing behind him. "I don't really know." Said Pam.

"Does he think Frank is here?" He asked

"He's not sure, we've been here over a week and this is the first he's mentioned anything like this."

"What are you going to do?"

"I don't know, sleep on it, I guess. Right now, I want to go shopping, I saw this area rug I want for my room. I'll be back soon. Leon make sure the boys don't go far." She grabbed her purse and was out the door. She headed straight for L.A. from Altadena. They had done a lot of driving around to familiarize themselves with the area, and the freeways. Sometimes with

Reggie, sometimes just the five of them. Pam liked driving and knowing her way around was important.

She found the post office and drove inside their private parking lot. It was around 2pm, she saw a few drivers and headed towards them. She got out of the car and walked over to one.

"Hi, she said, sorry to bother you, but have you ever seen this guy?" She showed him a picture. He shook his head and walked on. After 4 others said no, she was ready to give up. Another driver was just coming in, she waited for him. She showed him the picture, he looked and then took it. "I'm not sure. I know this guy they call Lucky, if you clean him up, give him a shave this could be him."

"Do you know where he is now?"

"No. He finds me on my route." He helps me out, and he's good at it. My back acts up sometimes, so I let him help and I give him $10 to $50 dollars a day depending on how much he does. I'm glad to help him, because I know he'll eat and/or get a room."

"He's a homeless man?" she asked shocked and sad.

"Seems like it to me."

"Will you see him tomorrow?

"Maybe, he got only $20 today. He considers $75 a week, is a good week. I didn't see him yesterday, so tomorrow is a good bet. He's not in any trouble, is he?"

"No, I'm looking for a missing friend, that may need my help. So, where do you see him?"

"You sure he's your friend?"

"Yes. I can offer him a permanent job. I only want to help him."

"Ok, you do look honest and pretty too. Can you be here at 7:30 in the morning? You can follow. Like I said, he finds me."

"Yes, I'll be here, and thank you."

Feeling elated, Pam left with a smile on her face and hope in her heart.

She arrived home and the first comment came from Lisa. "Ok, where is the rug?"

"Oh, I didn't get it, it was more than I expected. How's everything here?"

"Fine, Leon had a taste for fried chicken, mac and cheese, so I started cooking."

"Good, I'm beat. I'm going to lay down for a minute." Pam went to her room, laid on the bed and was out instantly. Pam woke up long enough to eat, shower, and kissed her boys, goodnight, before she was back in bed sleeping.

She got up the next morning excited. It was now 6am. She got dressed and left the house before anyone was up. Since there was no school or job to go to yet. She was at the post office by 7:15am, waiting for the mailman. A little while later she heard a knock on her window. "You ready," he yelled through the closed windows. "Let's go." They pulled out. Pam followed him for about 20 minutes before he got out to deliver his first piece of mail. She followed him for another six blocks, when out of nowhere a homeless man approached him. When they came back again to the back of the mail truck her heart leaped with joy. Frank it's Frank. She got out of the car and slowly walked towards them. Frank turned and saw her. "Hi, he said, anxious to get your mail?" he said it without a hint of recognition.

"No, she smiled. I'm looking for a handy-man, and I heard about you. Are you interested in a full-time, possibly live-in position?"

"Why me?"

"I heard you were a good guy, a hard worker, and an honest person. Just what I'm looking for. I just moved here, and I need work done in and around my house. Once you see what's to be done you can give me a price. What do you say? What's your name by the way?"

"People just call me Lucky."

"Ok Lucky, what do you say?"

"Well, I'm working now," he said looking at the mailman.

"Look Lucky, great chances don't come around often, you see one, you take it. I can do this job, don't worry about me."

"Ok lady, looks like you got a handy-man."

"Ok, let's go."

"I don't think I should get in your car in my condition, can I meet you somewhere?"

"Well let me think. Did I see a motel around here somewhere?"

"I'm not interested in getting lucky."

"Funny, I see where you got your name. No, I have a plan."

"There's a motel right down the street, not the greatest but it close. The mailman said. We pass it on our route, remember Lucky?"

"Yea, I remember."

"Ok, let's go."

"You sure?"

"Yes", I am not letting you out of my sight, she thought to herself. The mailman had some old newspapers and offered them to him. He took it and lined the back seat with it, and got in.

She got in the driver's seat and started up the car,

"Straight ahead?"

"Yes. This seems familiar, do we know each other?"

"If we've met, I'm sure we will figure it out sooner or later." They reached the place within 5 minutes. Even for a homeless person he didn't smell bad, he was just dirty. He must have been able to bath, regularly. She was thankful.

They got out to go book a room. Pam paid, with key in hand they went to the room. "Ok here is the plan. I have two sons, and I don't want them to be afraid of you. So, I need you to get cleaned up. She checked the bathroom to see what was in there and made a mental note of what to get. "Are you hungry?"

"A little, yes."

"What do you want?"

"Breakfast, and a coffee."

"Ok, relax, I'll be right back. You good? You will be here when I get back, right? I really do need your help."

"Yes, I want to help you, I'll stay put."

Pam left. She rode around until she spotted a drug store and a Burger King. She went to the drug store first grabbed soap, shampoo, toothbrush, toothpaste, razor, after shave, comb and brush. She checked out and went through the Burger King drive thru. She got a breakfast meal and a coffee for him and a breakfast sandwich and coffee for herself. She headed back to the room. Forty minutes had passed. She got to the door and knocked. She got no answer. She knocked again a little harder, still no answer. She panicked. She went to the front office and asked the guy to please open the door. He did. The first thing she heard was the shower. She relaxed. "Lucky!" She called out. "Yea!" He answered.

"I brought you better soap, can I bring it to you? Cover up." She went in the bathroom with her head down and handed him the soap. There is other stuff here, but if you want to eat first, before your food gets cold, it's here too. I'm leaving again and will be gone for about an hour. I will be back. "I've sized you up and I'm going to get clothes for you, Ok?"

"Ok, hey what's your name?"

"Pam, my name is Pam, Lucky."

"How old are your boys?"

"The oldest is 9, the younger one is 8."

"Big boys, I was thinking 2 & 3, since you are obviously having another one and real soon. When are you due?"

"In about two weeks."

"Should you be out here doing all this now, especially for a stranger?"

"Well this is important to me." she said. She had grabbed her sandwich and was almost finished. She drank a little coffee. Found she really didn't have a taste for it.

"I get that," he continued the yelling from one room to the other over the shower. "I guess you getting ready for the new one?"

"Yea, something like that." The water went off and Frank stepped out with a towel wrapped around him. The sight of him stirred up feelings she hadn't allowed herself to feel in a long time. She wanted to feel his arms around her, to hear him say 'my girl.' In time she reminded herself, in time. She looked away.

"The bed looked so inviting, but I didn't want to lay down all dirty, that's why I showered."

"Well, now you can eat and take a nap, she said. I am going to take the key, you didn't hear me when I got back, I got scared you'd changed your mind."

"I gave you my word, trust it. I'm trusting you."

"I'm glad." She walked to him and held out her hand. He took it. "Trust" they said together and smiled at each other.

"Anything in particular you want to wear?"

"Yes, clean drawers." They laughed.

"Eat, sleep. I'll be back in no time." She left.

It is now 8:45am, everyone is probably wondering where she is. She went to a phone booth and called home. Lisa was hysterical. "Where are you?"

"Sorry I should have left a note, but I have a surprise when I get home. Maybe around noon. Can you make sandwiches for lunch, tuna maybe?"

"Sure Pam, ok."

"Are the boys up?" Let me speak to them."

"Mommy?"

"Good morning baby, I'm fine just had something to do this morning. But I will be home for lunch Ok?" "Where's Joey?"

"Hey mommy."

"Hi baby, you sound so sweet. Are you being good?" "Yes mommy."

"Ok I will be home soon, don't worry ok?" "Ok mommy, bye."

"Bye baby."

"Pam?" Do you want tea for lunch?

"Sure, sounds good. Is Leon there? Tell him I want him home when I get there, ok?" "Ok." They hung up.

Pam knew where the Crenshaw Mall was, so she went there. There were stores closer, but she didn't know about them. It took a little longer than she expected but, it couldn't be help. She got there and found a store for men. She went in and bought underwear, t-shirt, two shirts, a pair of jeans and a pair of tan khakis. The shirts would match either pair of pants. Next, she went to a shoe store and bought socks and black tennis shoes. The shopping took over an hour. She got back to the room about 11:30. She went in. Frank or Lucky was asleep. His back was to her. She hated to wake him but, it had to be done.

"Hi sleepy head, wake up. Wake up!" she said a little louder. He stirred, then turned over. Her intake of breath did not go unnoticed.

"What, what's wrong?"

"Nothing, nothing at all. You just look so different all clean and shaven. You are quite a handsome man." He smiled.

"Thanks, lets see what you got pretty lady." She dumped everything on the bed.

"I like this stuff. For someone who doesn't know me, you know me." He picked up the jeans and a shirt and underwear and went to the bathroom. He came out smiling. "Perfect fit. You know what, before I went to sleep, I decided to tell you the truth about me. You deserve to know what you are getting into."

"What is it?"

"I don't know exactly who I am. I've been in this condition as far as I know for about a year. Don't know if I had an accident or running from the law. So, if you want to change your mind I will completely understand. You were right about how I got my name. I'd meet ladies, that want to help me, but it always came to an end when I tell them I'm not looking to get lucky. They'd do what you are doing and then send me on my way when I refuse to sleep with them. I agreed to help you but if you expect anything else, I won't do it. I need to know who I am."

"I understand, maybe a little stability will help. No, I don't want any more than was stated, so don't worry. So far you are everything you said you are, and I respect that. So as soon as you get dressed, we can get to the job and you can decide if you want it or not."

He finished dressing. "I have to say, no one has been as honest as you. I like that and I'm ready to go." He put the extra underwear, pants and shirt back in the bag along with the toiletries and walked to the door. They left. The drive was silent but nice for Pam. Feeling a weight had been lifted but unsure what would happen at the house. They pulled up to the house. She got to the door and opened it and look at Leon and Lisa sitting on the sofa. She put her finger to her lips and mouthed 'don't say nothing'. You understand?" They both nodded. Lucky had walked up behind her. She walked in saying I want you to meet Lucky. He's going to see if he wants to take the job of giving you a hand with what we want to do around here Leon. They both stood. Eyes wide and mouth open. These are my friends, the Kirkpatricks, Leon and Lisa.

"How are you?" Lucky said as he stuck out his hand to Leon. They shook. "I'm good and you?" He nodded.

He reached out to Lisa, "Ma'am." She shook his hand. They were looking at her for answers. "I heard about this nice guy out there, maybe could use a steady job, so I had to go see for myself. He agreed to check out the job, if he accepts, we will have a live-in worker."

"Have a seat Lucky, you might as well meet my boys. Let me get them." She went to their bedroom.

"Guys, I have someone here I want you to meet. Now listen, he doesn't know who he is yet so be cool. You know how to be cool?"

"Yes mommy" they assured her. "Come on", she grabbed their hands and held on.

They got to the living room and the boys stood there looking at their father for less than a second. They broke away from their mother's hand running full speed, yelling, "Daddy, daddy, you're home!"

Lucky grabbed them and said. "Hey Jr.! Hey Joey!" kissing them as he said their names. Surprising to everyone watching.

Now, Pam was the one with her mouth open and eyes wide.

"Let me look at you, Lucky said. You got bigger and handsome as ever."

"You too daddy, you look good". "Well that because your ...." realization hit hard. He said, "excuse me a minute, guys." He got up walked to Pam and said, "how in the hell did I not know you? My life, my love, my girl. I'm home, I'm finally home. Thank you, Jesus."

Then another realization, he turned and looked at Leon and Lisa. Hey man, I see you finally got a bun in the oven. By this time, they had got up and walked over to give him a proper hello. They embraced, first Leon, then Lisa, giving her a kiss and congratulations. "Thank you," said Lisa.

While he was greeting them, Pam had gone to the phone to call Reggie.

"Hey Reggie, he's here. I found him. Yes, yes, ok, when? Ok see you then." Everyone had resumed their seats. The boys crowding their father on the love seat. Leon and Lisa back on the sofa.

"So, who is Reggie?" asked Frank. "My friend from high school. Remember me telling you about him?" Pam replied. "Vaguely. So, tell me everything, it's like the last year of my life is a blur. Start with the baby." "You're going to have another son daddy, said Jr. Mommy fainted right after you left, and we made her go to the doctor. She found out she was pregnant. She was sad, a lot, because we couldn't find you." Pam had sat on the other side of Jr. while Joey was still in his father's lap. Frank reached over, his arm on the back of the sofa and caressed her neck and said, "Sorry babe". "So, we are in LA right? How did you guys get here.

"Let's wait till Reggie gets here, then we can go from there. That way you will know more and will be able to answers our questions too. In the meantime, Leon take, umm, what's your name." "Frank, my name is Frank, Pam." "Take Frank up and show him the job."

"You really weren't kidding about the job?"

"No, honesty, and trust remember.

"I love you."

"Love you too Lucky." The guys went upstairs.

Pam and Lisa went into the kitchen to finish lunch. Lisa had started the tea but wanted Pam to finish. So, Lisa made the sandwiches and Pam made the tea. They found chips and called the men down to eat. They all sat in their usual order. Frank at the far end, at the head which is a straight eye line to the front door with just a slight right turn of his head, Pam to his left, Jr. to his right, Joey to Jr. right, Leon at the head of the other end with Lisa to his right and to Lisa's right was Pam.

"Grace," said Pam. "Let's hold hands" said Frank. Grace was said and Amen by all.

Reggie arrived an hour later. He came on his lunch hour. As Pam opened the door for him a puppy dashed in leaving dirty paws all over the place.

"Can we keep him mommy?" The boys wanted to know.

"Oh, I thought he was yours. He was just laying by the door like he belongs here." Said Reggie.

"He's from next door, their dog had puppies, this one likes to play with us. "Can we keep him?" The boys asked again.

"For now, take him out back, we can talk to the neighbors later. It is imperative.."

"To keep the noise down, we know, come on Joey." Said Jr.

"Question!" Reggie said to Pam. "What is today's date?"

Pam looked at the calendar and said, "oh my goodness 17, and I am past my due date."

"Frank I am so very glad to meet you. I know you are anxious to get this over with. I am Reggie, a friend of Pam's from high school. Did they tell you anything?"

"No, it was almost like they were afraid to."

"Understandable. I am a psychic and a hypnotist. What I want to do is hypnotize you to bring you up to date as much as possible then we can clear up everything else, OK?"

"Is this necessary?" Frank asked.

"We all had to do it Frank. You are going to be totally surprise what you find out." said Leon.

"Pam?" "It's quite necessary darling." She said.

"Ok, let's get started."

Reggie took Frank under. "Now Frank go back to the last time you spoke to or was with Clinton, tell me about it." "I called him right after I spoke with Pam to find out why he was at my house. He told me to come over he needed my help with something. I went. As soon a I walked in, I heard these familiar sounds. He guided me to a chair and proceeded to tell me that he was in love and told me I had to pick out of the bowl and go where it said, and if I ever encountered the bottom, all would be as it was again. The top said California, the bottom said, my kids running into my arms, happy to see me."

"You didn't feel any resistance against the suggestion?"

"No, I felt powerless, this was something I had to do."

"No further instructions were given to you, as far as your survival was concerned?"

"No, my first shelter was under a bridge. I sat confused for hours, for days. I guess my own survival instincts took over. I did odd jobs, and was grateful for the kindness of others."

"Ok Frank, tell me about the last time you were with the other guys, what was expected of you?" "To convince girls to take out their ATM card and give us their pin number. It was too easy, You get their birth date, or address and play with the numbers, they would eventually, just tell you what it was." "Anything else?" "On a few occasions, one of us would go with him, if he had two different banks to hit.'

"Ok Frank I'm going to bring you out by counting back from 5. When I get to 1, you will open your eyes and remember everything you just said. Are we clear?" "Yes." And, you will not be able to get hypnotized again by Clinton. Understood?" "Yes." 5.. 4.. 3.. 2..1

Frank opened his eyes. "That's why you hit your wife? You were hypnotized?"

"Yes."

"I am the reason I was without you for the last seven months. It was all my fault. If I hadn't called you, you wouldn't have found yourself in this situation."

"This is in no way your fault. Let's keep the blame where it belongs. On Clinton! What happened to him?"

"He spent about eight months in prison and had to pay each victim $1,500." Said Leon.

"That's it? Did you guys kick his ass?" He asked Leon. "No, by the time we found out, the police had already picked him up."

"This is unbelievable. To know that a friend, of many years could do this to me, to us and our families is unacceptable. He needs to pay."

"Even though I was in a big city like Los Angeles, I felt like I was trapped in a canyon. A lot of room to roam but none of it made sense and there was no understanding. I had this continuous feeling that something or someone was missing."

"You and your wife were feeling the same. She too felt like she had been dropped in a canyon, with no way out. She felt lost, alone, and helpless without you. It was sad to see."

Frank got up and went to his wife and held her in his arms. He had no words, for right now, holding her was all he wanted to do. He felt his baby kick. Then heard Pam grunt. He looked at her face and knew, he was about to be the father of child number three. He thought, how great it was to be out of the canyon and into the deepest love he will ever know.

CPSIA information can be obtained
at www.ICGtesting.com
Printed in the USA
BVHW031045220819
556529BV00005B/23/P